"Oh, no. . .no. . ."

Confused, Risa looked at one of the young faces peering back at her. The boy appeared no older than fifteen. "Don't worry, Ma'am," he said. "Our pastor and another man just took off after the creeps who robbed you."

"My friend. . ." She choked, realizing tears were streaming down her cheeks. "She needs a doctor."

"I called for an ambulance," a female voice announced from somewhere.

Risa felt numb, dazed. She gathered Kari's unconscious form into her arms. "Please wake up," she pleaded, pushing back her girlfriend's blond hair, now soaked with blood.

She heard a man's voice. "We couldn't catch them." He sounded winded. . .and familiar. Lifting her gaze from Kari, she scanned the group until her bleary line of vision came to rest on none other than Mike Gerardi.

Risa closed her eyes, feeling dizzy and sick. This had to be a nightmare. The next thing she knew, she felt someone touching her shoulder. She looked up to see Mike hunkering beside her.

"Risa? Is that you?"

All she could manage was a weak nod. . . .

ANDREA BOESHAAR was born and raised in Milwaukee, Wisconsin. Married for twenty years, she and her husband Daniel have three adult sons. Andrea has been writing for over thirteen years, but writing exclusively for the Christian market for six. Writing is something she loves to share, as well as helping others develop. Andrea stays at home, takes care of her family, and writes.

HEARTSONG PRESENTS

Books by Andrea Boeshaar
HP188—An Uncertain Heart
HP238—Annie's Song
HP270—Promise Me Forever
HP279—An Unexpected Love
HP301—Second Time Around
HP342—The Haven of Rest
HP359—An Undaunted Faith
HP381—Southern Sympathies
HP401—Castle in the Clouds
HP428—An Unmasked Heart

Books under pen name Andrea Shaar
HP79—An Unwilling Warrior

Risa's Rainbow

Andrea Boeshaar

Heartsong Presents

To my Italian friends Cathy, Prudy, Roselle, and Marie. . .
Friends since grade school,
Friends forever!

A note from the author:
I love to hear from my readers! You may correspond with me
by writing: **Andrea Boeshaar**
Author Relations
PO Box 719
Uhrichsville, OH 44683

ISBN 1-58660-482-1

RISA'S RAINBOW

All Scripture quotations, unless otherwise noted, are taken from
the King James Version of the Bible.

All of the characters and events in this book are fictitious. Any
resemblance to actual persons, living or dead, or to actual events
is purely coincidental.

Cover illustration by Jocelyne Bouchard.

PRINTED IN THE U.S.A.

one

It's not fair.

On Thanksgiving Day, Risa Vitalis glanced across Nana Mandelini's formally set dining-room table with its pearly-white, lacy cloth and stared at her cousin, Annamarie.

"Isn't it exciting?" the petite brunette asked, holding out her left hand and waving a sparkling diamond engagement ring at Risa. "I'm getting married!"

"Iza 'bout time," Nana remarked with her heavy Italian accent. "How long have you been seeing thisa man? Two years? Iza 'bout time he makes you hisa wife."

Annamarie frowned at their grandmother's terse reaction, but Risa couldn't help a little smile. She felt the same way. It seemed that Annamarie and Tony had been dating forever. It *was* time they got married. Risa was ecstatic that it was finally happening, but at the same time, her heart ached because her younger cousin would be married first.

"Of course, I want you to stand up in my wedding, Risa," Annamarie said, peering across the platter of turkcy. Her dark brown eyes shone with anticipation. "Will you?"

"I'd be honored," she replied sincerely. She and her cousin had been as close as siblings since they were little girls.

"We don't want to wait very long, so we're planning a February wedding." She smiled dreamily. "Valentine's Day."

"Three months from now?" Risa exclaimed. "But I heard it takes years to plan a decent wedding. Reception halls are booked that far in advance."

"True, but we're not planning a typical ceremony and reception," Annamarie explained. "Valentine's Day is on a Thursday, and, well, we're going to have the reception in one

5

of the wedding chapel's banquet halls. I'll admit, a generic chapel and banquet hall aren't my first choice, but—"

"On a Thursday?" Risa hadn't gotten past that much yet. "I'll have to work."

"It's in the evening. You'll be done by seven, won't you?"

"Yeah, but. . ." She shook her head. "I'll see if I can work a half-day. I haven't even started my new job yet, and already I'm asking for time off."

"It'll work out, Risa. You'll see."

She had her doubts. "What kind of a reception are you planning?"

"A simple one. Hors d'oeuvres, wedding cake, punch, coffee. . ."

"What, no dinner?" Nana protested. "Annamarie, you gotta feeda your guests."

"They'll be fed. You'll love this wedding, Nana. I promise."

"Yah, we'll see," the older woman grumbled.

Risa thought it all over. "You know, this does sound a bit hasty. I've never heard of anyone planning a wedding in three months. . .unless it's held at the courthouse."

"Hey, Annamarie, are you afraid Tony will change his mind?" Uncle Vito joked from the other end of the table. "You gotta either nab him now or never, eh?" He chuckled while Nana gave her son a stern look. But obviously Uncle Vito wasn't finished with his wisecracks yet. "Hey, Risa, when you gettin' married? The Twelfth of Never?"

She lifted a brow. "Very funny."

He laughed in spite of his cheeks bulging with turkey and mashed potatoes.

"Risa's smart, Vito," his blond wife spouted. "She's staying single."

"What, you got something against being married?"

"I'll answer your question this way," his wife, Sharon, said. "If I knew then what I know now. . ."

"Yeah, well, I could say the same thing, you know?"

Nana rattled off a reprimand in Italian and Vito didn't say another word. Sharon, the only non-Italian at the dinner table, smirked as she lifted a thick slab of bread from her plate and took a bite. In the years that she'd been married, Sharon had learned to hold her own—with her husband and Nana too. In Risa's mind, Sharon had earned her place in the Mandelini family. . .unlike Risa's father, Nick Vitalis. Although he was Italian, he wanted nothing to do with the Mandelinis. The divorce between him and Risa's mother, Clarissa, had ended bitterly. Only a year later, Clare remarried.

And that's when the nightmare began for Risa.

Bill Walker, her stepfather, had been an abusive alcoholic, and Nana's house became a refuge where Risa learned to cook, bake, and forget all her troubles. But the year she entered high school, the violence in her own home increased and Risa was sent to live with her natural father. He made sure she got the counseling she needed to heal from the physical and emotional abuse she'd suffered at her stepfather's hand. However, Nick Vitalis vowed never to forgive the Mandelinis for allowing such mistreatment of his daughter. He claimed that *someone* should have stopped it. Risa might be inclined to agree, except back then she didn't talk about her home life much. No one really knew enough about her stepfather's cruelty to stop it.

Nevertheless, the war had begun, and the Vitalis family still hated the Mandelini family, and vice versa. In fact, they had hated each other for at least a decade, and Risa often found herself torn in two. After all, she loved both sets of grandparents, aunts, uncles, and cousins. Fortunately, she was a good mediator and managed to split her time and affections in a way that was acceptable to everyone. What's more, she'd learned to avoid her stepfather at holidays and family get-togethers.

But out of her dozens of relatives, Risa felt the closest to Nana Mandelini, her mother's mother. Ever since Risa was a little girl, Nana seemed to know her heart and sense her needs before Risa even knew they existed.

"She'll marry when she findsa the perfect man," Nana told Vito with a decisive nod of her gray head.

"There's no such thing," Risa countered.

"This iza true, but when you finda him, he will be perfect for you. Just like my Anthony wasa perfect for me, God rest his soul."

Risa glanced down at her dinner plate. More than a year ago, she'd thought for sure she had found the man for her: Wren Nickelson. Had he been Italian, he would have been "perfect." He had been her coworker at the post office. Divorced and having partial custody of his two young daughters, Risa had fallen in love with him because of his caring and sensitive nature. He was gallant and charming and so different from any man Risa had ever met. But it soon became apparent that Wren hadn't ever stopped loving his ex-wife, and he ended up marrying her—again.

Risa shook herself. No use dwelling on the past. Besides, she'd learned that loving someone, even as a friend, included looking out for his happiness, and Wren was certainly happy now that he and Nancie were back together.

"You needa to go to Italy and find a man," Nana said. From her place across the table, Annamarie chuckled.

Glaring at her cousin, Risa turned to her grandmother and replied, "I'm not that desperate, Nana, but thanks for the suggestion."

"Yah, I think you shoulda go to Italy," the old woman repeated. She gazed off in the direction of the living room, but Risa could tell she was miles away. It was then that she noticed the determined glint in her grandmother's rheumy hazel eyes, and Risa suspected that she would soon be planning a trip.

❧

Mike Gerardi set the telephone receiver back in its cradle

before reclining in his desk chair. He put his hands beneath his head and gazed up at the ceiling. Risa didn't answer her phone.

He sighed and grew pensive. Why did he have to take such an interest in Risa Vitalis anyway? Sure, she was a knockout with her carrot-orange hair that fell past her shoulders in an attractive tangle of curls. She had a curvy figure that Mike didn't like to admit he noticed, except he did. In short, he was attracted to her. But besides her physical attributes, Risa had spunk, a fun-loving spirit, and a sarcastic wit that made him laugh. She knew some of the same people he did, since Milwaukee's Italian community was a small, closely knit group. Most of all, his family would adore her.

However, it was Risa's honesty that truly impressed him—and, ironically, her honesty was what hurt him the most. It had been nothing short of love at first sight for him, but Risa made it clear in more ways than one that she wasn't interested in him or his "religion." No doubt she had checked her Caller ID before answering the phone this afternoon. Seeing it registering as someone from Bay Community Church, she didn't pick up, that is, if she were even at home. . . .

So why do I keep trying? he wondered.

Suddenly a passage from the second book of Corinthians flitted across his mind. *"What fellowship can light have with darkness? What harmony is there between Christ and Belial? What does a believer have in common with an unbeliever?"*

"Nothing, nothing, nothing," Mike said aloud as he stood. He felt suddenly discouraged, but he knew he should just drop the entire matter in God's hands. After all, the Lord loved Risa more than he ever would.

A knock sounded on his door.

"C'mon in."

Kevin Batzler, the senior pastor, strode into the office.

"Hey, Kev, how's it going?"

The man grinned. "I got an offer for you that you can't refuse," he said hoarsely, doing a bad imitation of Marlon

Brando in *The Godfather*.

Mike chuckled. "Yeah, yeah, I've heard that before."

Kevin sobered. "You know, I never did see that movie."

"Lucky you." Mike laughed again. "So, what's up?"

Kevin combed his fingers through his sandy-colored hair. "It's the upcoming mission trip. As you know, our youth group has been planning to tour the Holy Lands."

"Yeah. . .and?"

"Well, now plans have changed. Because of the recent terrorism in the Middle East, the kids—with a lot of prompting from their parents—voted to tour Italy instead."

"I think that's wise," Mike said. He'd been concerned about the missions endeavor after hearing of the latest acts of violence in Israel.

"I agree," Kevin replied. "So, here's the offer. . . . How about you take the youth group to Italy and I'll stay home?"

"You got something against Italy?" Mike asked facetiously.

Kevin grinned. "Hardly. In fact, you can't breathe a word of this to Julie." He shook his head. "If my wife finds out I turned down a trip to Italy, I'll be sleeping in the doghouse."

"Gotcha. My lips are sealed." Mike tipped his head. "So, why don't you want to go?"

Kevin's grin faded. "I've got too many responsibilities here. Like Lyle Campson, for instance. He's still in the intensive care unit, and it doesn't look good. I can't just take off now and leave the whole family. . . . I mean, I suppose I could. I have a terrific staff. But I don't want to. I feel accountable to this family since I've been the Campsons' pastor for ten years."

"I understand." Mike had only been the associate pastor at Bay Community Church for two years and already he felt "accountable" to various members of his congregation. "Although," he added in afterthought, "things could change in the next two or three weeks. Maybe you can still go."

Kevin shook his head. "I have a feeling I'm only going to

get busier. Our Christmas program is right around the corner."

Mike nodded thoughtfully.

"So what do you think? Italy? You speak the language. . . ."

"Well, sort of," Mike replied. "My Italian isn't the best. But I'd love to see what my grandfather used to refer to as 'the old country.' I've never been there, and I've always wanted to go."

"Great. Your prayers have been answered," Kevin said with a light of amusement in his gray-blue eyes. "Start packing. Get your passport in order. In a few short weeks, you'll be on your way to spending ten days in Italy."

❧

"It's now or never, Risa. Either you go on that trip now, or you might never get the chance."

As they strolled through the mall on the last day of November, she wondered if her friend Kari was right. Now might be the perfect time to visit Italy. It had become Nana's fervent wish that she do so, and Risa's appetite had been whetted by her grandmother's stories of "back home by the sea." Additionally, Risa was between jobs, and after she started her new career January 1 at a large insurance company downtown, she wouldn't be entitled to vacation time until after she'd been on the job for a year. During that twelve-month period, her financial situation could change, and she might not have the money.

"Are you still thinking about coming along?" Risa queried, looking askance at her blond friend.

"You kidding? That's all I've been thinking about since you brought up the subject a couple of weeks ago. José said he'd watch Jodi while we're gone," Kari added, referring to her former boyfriend and their two-year-old daughter. "That's a miracle, since the jerk said he didn't want anything to do with her. . .or me." Kari let go of a long sigh, and Risa could tell the situation hurt her friend more than she would ever tell. "Can you imagine all the fun we'd have if we toured Italy?"

"We'd shop till we drop," Risa said with a grin.

"For sure. And I heard Italian men are fascinated by American women," Kari said, her blue eyes sparkling with mischief. "That's you and me, Ris. . .fascinating American women."

She laughed. "Right."

"Hey, speaking of fascinating," Kari said on a note of sarcasm, "does that pastor still call you and ask you to come to his church?"

"Mike?" Risa shook her head. "Nope. Haven't heard from him in a few weeks. I think he finally gave up on me."

"About time."

Risa grinned. "That's an Italian man for you, Kari. Stubborn and persistent. Can't take no for an answer."

"My kind of guy. . .just as long as he's not a pastor. I mean, I always think of those guys as killjoys. No fun, just read their Bibles and point out the error of your ways. Life with a pastor has got to be big-time *boring*. Think about it."

"I have." In truth, Risa had enjoyed having dinner with Mike the one and only time they'd gone out together. Paradoxically, the purpose of that "date" had been to talk about Wren. He'd decided to go back to his ex-wife, much to Risa's disappointment. Mike had deliberately postponed their discussion until after they'd lingered over a lovely dinner. But then he'd taken Wren's side, furthering Risa's frustration. It wasn't that she wanted to be a home-wrecker. The "home" had already been wrecked in her opinion. Wren was divorced, and she would have never considered falling in love with him otherwise.

"You considered dating the guy?"

"Who, Mike? Sure I did, for about ten minutes. . .before I figured out the good pastor wasn't interested in me romantically. He was just looking for his next convert."

"If that's true, it stinks. Then again, guys always have an ulterior motive for pursuing a woman, don't they? They always want something, whether it's a convert or a conquest. Men can never think in terms of forever when it comes to relationships."

Risa contemplated the remark as she and Kari entered a large department store. They headed for the cosmetic and perfume counter, where Kari purchased her favorite scent. Then they strolled over to the jewelry and gazed at the gold and silver necklaces, bangles, and diamond rings.

"Hey, is Wren still happily married?"

Risa nodded. "Yep."

"Bummer."

After a moment's deliberation, Risa shook her head. "No, not really. I never thought it would happen, but I can honestly say that in the past eighteen months, I've gotten over Wren, and. . .and I'm actually happy for him and his wife."

"You are unreal," Kari quipped, shaking her head. "I think that pastor is rubbing off on you more than you know."

Risa chuckled under her breath. "Yeah, right."

Kari turned from the counter and gave her a hard stare. "Know something? I need this vacation, Ris," she said. "Look at me. I'm a hard-working single mom with vacation time coming, and, like the song goes, 'love's been a little bit hard on me.' "

"Make that 'us.' " Risa couldn't think of one time when love *hadn't* been hard on her.

"Come on," Kari continued, "let's go to Italy and make some memories that'll last for years. We owe it to ourselves to turn the tables for once. We'll be the American heartbreakers."

Her smile broadened. Kari could talk her into almost anything. "All right," she said at last, "let's go."

two

Risa breathed in the fresh sea air as she and Kari dined at a sidewalk café. Even in December, the weather proved to be bright and balmy. So far, it had been the perfect vacation. Italy was everything the travel agent had promised and more. They had toured Venice, Florence, and Rome—where they'd celebrated Christmas—before spending their last four days here in Palermo, Sicily. Frequently called *"la brutta e la bella"* or "the ugly and the beautiful," the city offered spectacular historical sites as well as some not-so-spectacular views, such as overcrowded conditions in certain areas and horrible traffic jams. And then there were the infamous pickpockets.

Still, the museums were fascinating, the restaurants excellent, and the men. . .well, all of them had been very polite except for the jerks who presently sat with them. The pair just couldn't seem to understand that she and Kari weren't interested in whatever they were offering. . .which neither Risa nor Kari could fully comprehend. While Risa knew a bit of Italian, enough to get her to a restaurant, hotel, or the ladies' bathroom, Kari couldn't say more than *"arrivederci"*—and, obviously, that word wasn't in these fellas' vocabularies.

Kari leaned over and whispered, as if the men could understand English, "Risa, try again to tell these dudes to get lost. Maybe this time they'll get it."

With a sigh of frustration, Risa attempted the task once more. When that didn't work, she fished her travel-size English/Italian dictionary from her purse and looked up the words, rolling them around her tongue before speaking aloud. *"Andare via,"* she said carefully. Then she pointed to herself and Kari. *"Non interessato."*

14

"That sounded good," Kari said. "Even I understood that last part. What else did you say?"

"I told them to go away, that we're not interested."

"Perfect."

Risa and Kari gave the two dark-haired men expectant stares. Risa thought the one on her right had kind of a baby face, all pudgy with pimply skin, but the other's looked hard, with his scruffy beard and beady, ebony eyes. He gave Risa the creeps.

The men conversed briefly before standing. Then the frightening-looking one balled his fist and shook it in the air while rattling off a series of words that sounded quite menacing.

"Do you think he's threatening us?"

"Don't know," Risa replied. "He's probably cussing us out. But who cares? They're leaving."

Kari heaved an audible sigh of relief. "Good. But now I need some more *vino.*" She raised her hand and waved to their waiter. "*Garçon, garçon. . .*"

Risa rapped her friend on the arm. "That's French, you nut!"

"Oops, wrong country."

Collapsing against the back of her chair, Risa laughed.

❧

A good while later, Risa and Kari ambled their way back to the hotel, singing a Dean Martin oldie about moonlight in eyes, big pizza pies. . .and "amore-ey." As they turned the corner, two men suddenly stepped out of the shadows, blocking their way. Risa instantly recognized them as their incorrigible dinner guests of earlier in the evening. The tough-looking one said something in a demanding tone of voice.

"What does he want?" Kari asked.

"I don't know," Risa replied.

He repeated it.

Kari boldly faced him. "It's like we said before, Dude. . .no speaka Italiano." She waved her arms and looked so silly that Risa started laughing.

The man began to shout.

Risa swallowed her mirth, and sheer fright took its place. These guys weren't kidding around.

"Go away!" Kari shouted, obviously feeling panicked too.

Risa looked around for someone—anyone who might help. However, in the next moment, the unthinkable occurred. The beady-eyed man stepped forward and delivered a powerful blow to the side of Kari's head. She spun around like a toy soldier before dropping to the ground. Risa stood there, stunned. Then the other man lunged toward her. Her survival instincts took over and she kicked him and screamed, but despite her best efforts, he got close enough to yank the gold necklace from around her neck. He then proceeded to pull the earrings from her lobes. Risa slapped, kicked, and scratched at his face, but he continued to seize her jewelry, her watch and gold bracelet, the blue star sapphire ring her grandmother had given her for her twenty-first birthday. He ended the assault by pushing her hard against the side of a brick building and snatching her purse.

And then he was gone. So was his crony.

Shaken, Risa turned to her friend. Much to her horror, she found Kari lying face down in a pool of blood.

"Oh, no. . .no. . ." She knelt beside her, turning her over and cradling her head. "Kari? Kari, please say something."

Seconds seemed like eternity as Risa tried to think of what she could do, where she could summon help. The next thing she knew, a small crowd stood around her. . .an English-speaking crowd. Where had they come from?

Confused, Risa looked at one of the young faces peering back at her. The boy appeared no older than fifteen. "Don't worry, Ma'am," he said. "Our pastor and another man just took off after the creeps who robbed you."

"My friend. . ." She choked, realizing tears were streaming down her cheeks. "She needs a doctor."

"I called for an ambulance," a female voice announced from somewhere.

Risa felt numb, dazed. She gathered Kari's unconscious form into her arms. "Please wake up," she pleaded, pushing back her girlfriend's blond hair, now soaked with blood.

She heard a man's voice. "We couldn't catch them." He sounded winded. . .and familiar. Lifting her gaze from Kari, she scanned the group until her bleary line of vision came to rest on none other than Mike Gerardi.

Risa closed her eyes, feeling dizzy and sick. This had to be a nightmare. The next thing she knew, she felt someone touching her shoulder. She looked up to see Mike hunkering beside her.

"Risa? Is that you?"

All she could manage was a weak nod. . . .

And then the ambulance arrived.

&

Sitting in the hospital's waiting area, Risa accepted the cup of coffee Mike handed her and then watched from the corner of her eye as he settled into the chair beside her. With his assistance in speaking Italian, she'd been able to communicate to the police about what had happened and to describe the assailants. Nevertheless, she wished Mike would go away, not because she didn't appreciate his help, but because he always seemed to catch her at her worst.

The last time they had seen each other, Risa was pining over Wren Nickelson. It had been her hope that Mike, being one of Wren's pastors, would talk some sense into him. At dinner with Mike, she had explained her take on the situation; but instead of seeing it her way, he tried to show her several passages in the Bible to help explain Wren'sbeliefs—and his. Mike even mentioned "adultery," although Risa couldn't exactly recall the context in which he'd used the word. Nevertheless, it had totally crushed her, because that's obviously the way he viewed her—like some sleazy woman after a happily married man. But it hadn't been that way at all. Wren had been divorced at the time. He wasn't married.

And tonight, she had probably sunk even lower on Mike's scale of virtues. He wasn't dumb. He knew she'd consumed a few glasses of wine with dinner, something any noble pastor would frown upon. . .wouldn't he?

Just her luck; she wasn't even safe from running into Mike Gerardi in another country! And why did she care how he viewed her, anyway?

"So when did you arrive in Palermo?" the object of her tumultuous thoughts asked.

"Almost a week ago." She sipped her hot coffee. "And you?"

"About ten days. I'm traveling with eight kids and three adults from church."

"Mmm-hmm. . ." A church function. She should have known.

"We've been helping one of the missionaries we support," Mike continued, "so it's been a lot of work as well as fun. But the next two days are purely pleasure before we head for home."

Mike sat back and crossed his legs in a way that made his left knee stick out close to her hand that held the coffee.

She switched hands. "You don't have to wait around. I'm sure you've got things to do. But thanks for your help."

"The teens and other chaperones will survive without me for awhile."

So will I, Risa thought sarcastically, as her head began to throb. She took another sip of her coffee.

"I'm sorry about your friend, but I think it's good news that she regained consciousness in the ambulance."

Risa agreed.

"What about you? You okay?"

"I'm fine," she said. "Just a bruised ego, if anything."

She kept her eyes averted; she didn't want to see whether Mike smiled or frowned at the reply. And she certainly didn't need a sermon on the evils of alcohol. If anyone could preach it, she could. Her stepfather was a drunk. But she was different. Risa only indulged on occasion, and she never beat anybody up! She was hardly an alcoholic. But Mike would probably assume otherwise.

"I don't have a drinking problem." The words were out as the argument simultaneously flitted through her head, and they sounded defensive to her own ears.

"Glad to hear it."

"Kari and I just had a little wine with dinner."

"Risa, you don't owe me any explanations."

"No, but that's probably what you think. You think I'm some big lush." Guilt caused her tone to be sharper than she intended. She looked over at Mike in time to see an expression of puzzlement waft across his dark features.

She quickly turned away.

"I could never think badly of you."

Yeah, right, Risa thought. But there was a note of sincerity in his voice that she couldn't deny.

"Besides, I've been there. Years ago, I'd get plastered every weekend, and I didn't have a drinking problem."

Now it was her turn at surprise. "You? Drunk?" She couldn't envision it.

Mike grinned. "Do you think I've lived a perfect life or something?"

"Well, you're a pastor."

"Doesn't mean I'm perfect. Although, I will admit that I drank during my college days. . .before I came to know Christ."

"So *now* you're perfect."

He chuckled. "Far from it. I'm a sinner saved by grace. But I'm still a sinner, like anyone else."

Risa narrowed her gaze. "But you don't get drunk anymore."

"No. . .no, I don't."

"So in your book, it's a sin."

"In my opinion, drunkenness is sin in God's Book too. I

could sit here and quote you Bible verse after Bible verse, but I won't. . .unless you ask me to. But my point is this: There are plenty of evils associated with alcohol, so Christians are wise to stay away from it."

Risa couldn't argue with him about the "evil" part. Rising from her chair, she walked to the far end of the waiting room and pretended to study the candy machine. All the while, she sifted through her thoughts and sipped her coffee.

Mike Gerardi was a hard guy to figure out, and he sure wasn't like any clergyman Risa had ever met. He seemed like any other man—and one she might be attracted to, except for his religion. That part about him turned her off, mostly because she knew she couldn't live up to God's standards. . .or Mike's, either. But the fact that he admitted to getting drunk in the past shed new light on his character and made him seem. . .human. All this time, she'd imagined Mike had grown up in some kind of a monastery.

Pivoting, she chanced a look in his direction and found that he'd picked up a magazine. His dark head was bent slightly forward as he leafed through the pages. He had a natural olive skin tone that was darkened further by the sun. His red polo shirt seemed to enhance his broad shoulders and tanned forearms, while his legs were encased in blue jeans. On his feet he wore white athletic shoes with blue trim.

In Risa's summation he was a handsome man, but good looks could get a guy only so far. There had to be something more, something deeper. At least that's what she craved in a romantic relationship. Besides, she knew from her religious conversations with Wren that born-again Christians couldn't get romantically involved with people who didn't believe the same way. Risa always thought that was sort of insulting. They sure had lofty opinions of themselves, those born-agains.

As if sensing the weight of her stare, Mike looked up. His brown-eyed gaze met hers for a long moment before Risa turned back to the candy machine.

"Need some change?" he called to her.

She shook her head. She didn't "need" anything Mike Gerardi had to offer. All she wanted was for Kari to be okay so they could get out of this hospital—out of this city—and resume their vacation, what was left of it, anyway.

At that precise moment, a well-groomed, heavyset man with blond hair entered the waiting area. He wore a white lab coat, and a stethoscope dangled around his neck. In a booming voice, he called Risa's name.

"I'm Risa Vitalis," she answered, striding toward him.

"Hi. I'm Dr. Cappella," he said, holding out his right hand, "and I speak English. Fluently."

"I'm very glad to hear it." Risa's smile of relief became a frown of concern. "How's Kari?"

"She's got a concussion, but she's going to be all right. I still want to keep her overnight for observation, though."

Risa nodded. "Sure."

Mike had made his way over and listened in on the conversation.

"You two together?" Dr. Cappella asked.

"Sort of," Risa replied. "This is Pastor Mike. . .the Good Samaritan."

"I'm Dr. Cappella." The two men shook hands. "Nice to meet you."

Mike nodded, but regarded the physician curiously. "Hey, don't I know you? Cappella. . .Joe Cappella? The guy who dated my sister Roselle?"

After a wide-eyed stare, a grin spread across his face. "Don't tell me you're Mike, Roselle Gerardi's younger brother?"

"That's me."

"Madman Mike?" He dropped his head back and laughed. "I'm surprised you're still alive." Smiling broadly now, Dr. Cappella glanced at Risa before turning back to Mike. "Did she just say you're a. . .a pastor?"

He chuckled. "She did, and it's the truth. God saved me,

then called me to the ministry. I'm here in Palermo with my youth group."

"Talk about miracles!"

"I'm a walking, talking miracle."

"I'd say that's right, considering where you were when I saw you last. It was in a pool hall on Milwaukee's east side, if I remember correctly. You'd gotten into a fight—"

"No kidding?" Risa couldn't believe her ears. She looked over at Mike and wondered how such a thing could be possible.

"Listen, Joe, we don't have to dredge up the gory details, okay?" Mike gave the doctor a pointed stare.

"Oh, right." He laughed, then waved his index finger between Mike and Risa. "So, how do you two know each other?"

"Risa and I had previously met through a mutual friend. Then tonight we ran into each other here in Sicily."

"Wow, what a coincidence."

"Yeah, I suppose. . ." Risa wanted to call it plain old bad luck, but she held her tongue.

"I hate to tell you, but I don't believe in coincidence," Mike announced. "I believe everything that happens has a purpose."

"Are you going to give us a sermon?" Risa asked, lifting a brow.

"Nope." Mike raised his palms in surrendered promise.

Dr. Cappella stood by, chuckling.

"So how do *you* two guys know each other?" Risa asked, returning the question.

"I went to med school in Milwaukee. That's how I know Mike and his family."

"Yep, he dated my sister," Mike added, "but then broke her heart and moved to Italy to marry some distant cousin."

The doctor shrugged. "What can I say? Our families had planned it when we were kids. I never meant to hurt Roselle."

"I know," Mike said with a grin.

"How is she, by the way?"

"Happily married with a pack of kids."

"Good for her. Gina and I have three children." Joe laughed. "And you'd better get started, old man, if you plan on being a father some day. . .or don't you guys—your order, that is—get married?"

"We can get married."

Risa felt decidedly uncomfortable with the topic—especially the part about having children. She looked over at the vending machine, distancing herself from the conversation. She figured she'd never have kids. Her biological clock was ticking, so when Kari asked her to be little Jodi's sponsor at the traditional dedication, Risa jumped at the chance. While it was true that Risa had plenty of nieces and nephews, it was also a fact that they were all well cared for, loved, and properly spoiled by grandparents, aunts, and uncles. Kari, on the other hand, didn't have the same support system, so Risa frequently baby-sat on weekends or overnight. . .whenever Kari needed the help.

"I'll bet you want to see your friend."

Risa swung her gaze back to the doctor and nodded. "Yes, I would."

He smiled. "Okay, follow me."

three

Risa followed Dr. Cappella into the emergency department, where they turned left and walked a few more steps into a curtained examination room. Kari lay sleeping on a gurney, an IV threaded into her arm. Her forehead was scraped and around her left eye, a dark, ugly bruise had already begun to form.

Grieved by the sight of her girlfriend's sorry state, Risa hurried to her bedside. "Kari?" She touched her arm and Kari's eyelids fluttered open.

"Ris. . ." Her lips curved upward in a groggy smile.

"Are you okay?"

"Sure. I had to get a few stitches in my head, though."

"Does it hurt?"

"No. That handsome doctor gave me some pain medication. Did you see him, Ris?"

"Um. . ." Embarrassed, she looked across the bed at the blond physician, who gave her an amused grin. "I take it you're referring to Dr. Cappella?"

"Right, that's him."

Risa swallowed a laugh. "He's standing right here, so watch what you say. He speaks English."

"I know," Kari replied with a sleepy smile. "I asked him how he could be Italian and have blond hair."

"And?" Risa chanced another look at the doctor.

"And, he sort of gave me a history lesson. He said the Norsemen had landed in Palermo before the time of William the Conqueror."

Risa grinned. "See? This vacation hasn't been for nothing," she teased. "You actually learned something."

"You're such a smart aleck."

Her words lacked their usual enthusiasm, but overall, Kari seemed her old self. Looking over at Dr. Cappella, Risa smiled. "She's just fine."

Beside her, Mike chuckled, and it was then that Risa realized he'd followed her into the room. By now, Kari had obviously become aware of his presence, too, as questions pooled in her blue eyes.

"Um, Kari. . .this is Mike Gerardi. I believe I've mentioned him before," she stated pointedly, hoping her friend would take the hint. "Mike happens to be here in Sicily with his youth group. They witnessed the mugging tonight."

"Mike. . .the pastor? That Mike?"

"That's me." He leaned slightly forward over the gurney. "Nice to meet you."

"Same here." She squinted hard. "But you don't look like a pastor."

Risa's grin broadened.

"I guess I imagined someone totally different," Kari murmured, her eyelids looking suddenly very heavy.

Risa watched Mike smile at the remark, and then Dr. Cappella excused himself, saying he had other patients waiting. Moments later, Kari dozed off into a peaceful sleep.

"I'm glad she's okay," Risa murmured, touching the top of Kari's hand.

"So am I."

An uncomfortable moment of silence passed between them.

"Have you and Kari known each other long?" Mike asked.

"A few years," she replied, peering down at her sleeping friend. "Kari worked at the postal station I managed. She'd been hired through a temporary service, but then got offered another job somewhere else. She took the position and left the post office, but the two of us kept in contact."

Mike's dark head nodded in understanding.

"Kari's got a little girl who's staying with her dad while she's on vacation," Risa continued. "I worried that Kari's head injury was a lot worse, and all I could think of. . ." Risa swallowed a rising sob. "All I could think of was poor little Jodi without a mother."

"Well, you can stop fretting," Mike assured her. "It looks like your friend is going to be just fine and out of the hospital by tomorrow."

Convinced that what he said was true, Risa turned and followed him out of the room. They paused by the entryway.

"Thanks for your help, Mike." She meant it sincerely.

"Anytime. Say, how 'bout we get a cup of coffee?"

Risa glanced across the waiting area at the wall clock. "If I drink coffee at this late hour, I'll be up all night."

"So will I. But you haven't lived until you've tasted the cappuccino at this little coffeehouse I found. Friends of my cousin Claudio own the place. Claudio told me to look them up when I got to Palermo, so I did. Wasn't sorry, either."

They reached an awaiting taxi, and Risa realized she'd gotten so caught up in Mike's rambling that she hadn't noticed he'd taken hold of her elbow and led her from the hospital. But she figured it couldn't hurt to have a cup of decaf with the guy, so she climbed into the backseat of the car. Besides, she was curious as to why Dr. Cappella had referred to him as "Madman Mike." And what was all this about a fight in a pool hall?

Mike got in, closed the car door, and gave the taxicab driver directions in Italian. The car lurched forward.

"Good job. So, do you speak fluent Italian?"

"Nope. Claudio, the cousin I mentioned before, gave me a crash course. He'd lived in Sicily most of his life, but came to the States because his brother—my other cousin—is getting married in February. So I told Claudio he could have the spare bedroom in my apartment if he taught me Italian. He agreed, and now I can converse somewhat, although my comprehension isn't good."

"I've got a cousin getting married in February too," Risa

murmured, "and I'm totally depressed about it."

"Why?"

"Because. . ." She bit off the rest of her reply. How could she say, "It should be me getting married, not Annamarie!" That sounded horribly selfish, and maybe it was. Regardless, Risa wasn't about to share her heart with Mike and get a sermon in return. "Oh, it's a long story," she finished lamely.

Mike chuckled. "Well, after this cappuccino, it'll be a long night. Trust me."

Minutes later, the taxi pulled to a stop and Mike climbed out. He extended his hand to Risa and helped her from the car, then paid the driver.

"I look a mess," she said, gazing down at her blood-stained, emerald-green silk shirt and tan pants.

"It's really not that noticeable, Risa."

"Oh yeah, right." She had to laugh.

"Hey, you'll be among friends. No one will care. . .except that you're all right after getting robbed tonight."

She glanced back at the taxi. "I don't know. . . ."

"Oh, c'mon." Mike opened the door, then waved her over.

After another moment of deliberation, Risa caved in to his request, mainly because she didn't feel like going back to the hotel yet. She stepped inside the coffeehouse, and Mike followed. He called a greeting to the man behind the counter, who shouted a welcome in return.

"Hey, Mama, Anthony, Maria. . .iza Mika Gerardi!"

Within a minute, half a dozen people poured out from all corners of the shop. The men slapped Mike on the back in a hearty reception, and a stout, gray-haired woman reached up with both hands and pinched his cheeks. Risa laughed, thinking that between his choppy Italian and his friends' broken English, they communicated quite well.

"This is Risa Vitalis," Mike announced, beginning the introductions. He then went on to explain that she and Kari had gotten mugged earlier. The group was immediately sympathetic.

"Come, sit," the older woman said, leading Risa over to a table near the counter. "I get you coffee."

"Decaf, please."

The woman nodded and strode off in the direction of the kitchen, and Risa wondered if she understood what "decaf" meant. Did they have that here in Sicily?

Mike soon joined her at the table, and the exuberance surrounding him waned. After a few more exchanges, his relatives went back to work.

"Charming little place, don't you think?" Mike asked.

Risa could only agree, as she noticed the gleaming white walls, forest green woodwork with red border, and the green-and-white-checked tile floor. White café curtains hung in each long, narrow window, and covering each of the tall, round-topped tables were red plastic cloths.

"Notice the pictures on the walls," Mike said. "They're historic photographs of Palermo."

"Really?" Risa stood to take a closer look at the artwork. She walked around the coffee shop. "My grandmother would love this place," she murmured, reclaiming her seat.

"Tell me about your family," Mike said, looking genuinely interested.

"Nothing much to tell, really," she replied. "My parents divorced and my mom got remarried. . .to the king of jerks. My dad's got a live-in girlfriend, and they've been together for years. I've got a half-brother, Joey, whom I haven't spoken to in about half a decade because he's a chip off the old block, if you know what I mean."

"Indeed I do, but in the opposite sense. I've got a few family members who won't talk to *me*."

"Why?" And then she guessed. "Because of your vocation?"

"Exactly. Now, as you were saying. . .you've got a half-brother. . . ."

"Right, and a million aunts, uncles, and cousins."

Mike chuckled softly. "I can relate to the millions of aunts, uncles, and cousins too. The number seems almost realistic when we all get together."

Risa smiled politely and watched a young, dark-haired woman walking toward them with two large mugs of frothy-topped cappuccino.

"This is decaf, right?" Risa asked as the ceramic mug was placed in front of her.

"Yah, I guesso." The waitress smiled at Mike. "Mama say 'on the house.' "

"*Grazie,*" he replied.

The woman walked away, and Risa took a sip of the hot, creamy brew. It didn't taste like decaf, but she didn't feel right about voicing a complaint. Rather, she felt grateful it was "on the house," since she didn't have a dime on her. Having had her purse stolen, Risa was only too glad she'd left her credit cards and passport back at the hotel. All the thieves got tonight was a tube of lipstick, a makeup compact, a few sticks of gum, and several dollars. Her jewelry, on the other hand, was a substantial loss. She wondered how much Kari had had in her handbag.

"Mmm, this stuff is the best," Mike said.

Risa turned in time to see him take another sip of his cappuccino.

Looking over his mug, his eyes seemed to smile at her. And something else. . .

Risa looked back into her coffee. "Heard from Wren lately?" she couldn't help asking. And she really didn't mean anything by it. She was simply trying to quell the sudden discomfort she felt, sitting here with Mike.

"Um, yeah," Mike said between sips of his cappuccino. "He's a dad for the third time. Nancie gave birth to another girl. Sarah Joy."

"How nice. I'm happy for him. . .them."

"Pardon me for saying so, but you don't sound happy."

Risa sort of smirked. "Well, that has nothing to do with

Wren and everything to do with. . .with this whole night."

"Totally understandable."

"Besides," Risa continued, "there's someone out there for everyone, and Nancie was Wren's 'someone.' "

"I agree."

"But you know," she added, sitting back in her chair, "I've pretty much decided there's no one out there for me; marriage and a family just aren't going to happen."

"Oh, now, Risa—"

"No, really. And I'm not just feeling sorry for myself. It's not the booze talking here, either, because I honestly didn't drink that much. I've just come to accept the fact that I'm probably going to be single forever."

Again Mike didn't answer, and when Risa gazed his way, she found him staring thoughtfully into his mug.

"Maybe you can understand this, Mike, and maybe you can't. But, for me, nothing seems to turn out in the way of romantic relationships. Last week, for instance, a nice-looking, very polite guy asked me out to dinner. Before accepting, I asked him if he was married. . .and he was! 'Separated,' he called it." She shook her head. "I refused to date him. I never want to be in a situation where I'm the 'other' woman."

"Can't blame you for that."

"That role's not for me." She swatted at an errant tear, feeling suddenly embarrassed over the outburst. Perhaps the wine she'd consumed earlier did have something to do with her blubbering after all.

"Oh, hey, listen, thanks for coming to my pity party. But it's over now and I'll be fine. I always am."

"I can completely relate to your frustration. . .and your disappointment."

Surprised and curious all at once, she gave Mike her undivided attention. "You can? But you're a—"

"A pastor. You're right, I am. But I'm a single pastor who would like to get married some day."

Risa found that tidbit interesting. "So, are you. . .looking?"

"Nope," Mike said decisively. "I'm going to let God bring the right one to me."

"Good luck," Risa said.

"Thanks. But I don't need luck. I've got the Lord."

"Whatever."

Mike glanced over at her and smiled.

Risa found herself smiling back, but then her curiosity resurfaced. "So how come Dr. Cappella called you 'Madman Mike'?"

He groaned aloud. "Let's not go there, okay?"

"Oh, come on. I want to know."

Mike rubbed his jaw. "All right. . . . Well, most of my church members have heard my testimony, so what I'm about to tell you isn't any kind of dark secret."

"Okay."

After another sip of cappuccino, he began. "When I was in high school, I was a short little punk who thought that in order to be a man, I had to act tough. I picked fights with just about everyone. Except girls. I was sort of afraid of them— *intimidated* I guess would be the better word choice."

"Why?" Risa couldn't help but ask, wearing a grin. For some reason, she found Mike's past intriguing. Perhaps because it made him seem like a regular guy.

"Most girls were taller than I was," Mike replied, with a hint of a smirk. "I knew I couldn't impress them with my height and good looks, so I tried showing them how well I could fight. Little did I know," he said with a raised brow, "that they were not impressed in the least. If anything, it turned them off.

"Well, the summer after graduation, I surprised everyone, including myself, by growing two inches. By my junior year of college, I'd grown another two inches, resulting in my five feet, nine-and-a-half-inch height. I'm not a tall man, but I'll take five-nine over five-five any day."

He chuckled, and Risa laughed along.

"My last year of college, I met a young lady who was a born-again Christian. She fascinated me, but she didn't share my interest. She told me she wanted to be a missionary and that she wanted to marry a 'godly' man. I figured I didn't qualify, but back then, I didn't know why."

"Didn't you feel insulted?" Risa asked.

Mike thought it over. "No, not really. I just wanted to know what I had to do to get into that category. . .so I could get a date with her. Interestingly enough, Jenny never shared the gospel with me. She made me search things out for myself, and now I know why. If she had told me how to be born again, I would have prayed right then and there just so I could go out with her. Wrong motive. See, each of us has to come to Christ because His Holy Spirit is drawing us."

"Spare me the sermon, Pastor," Risa said, holding up a hand. "I've heard it before. Wren's told me, you told me, I heard it at your church that time I visited. . . ."

"Well, good. Now you're ready to make a decision."

"I'm not making any decision," she shot back. "And I certainly don't want to discuss it."

"All right, Risa. I'm sorry. I shouldn't have pushed you."

Ignoring the apology, she stood and strode toward the door. All she could think of was, *Get out and get as far away from Mike Gerardi as possible.*

She felt scared. She felt hunted, like a character in a movie she'd once seen, where aliens were after her, trying to force her to become one of them. They wanted her mind, her very being, and everywhere this character went, she ran into aliens who were disguised as humans. She couldn't trust anyone. . .not even the police.

That's how Risa felt. . .like she had to run for her life.

"Risa, hold on!"

Outside, she began to jog up the street with the chief alien on her heels. But he was faster and ran around in front of her, halting her progress.

"Whoa! Risa, where are you going?"

She tried to form an answer, but she hadn't a clue. She was in a foreign country with no money, and she hadn't any idea in which direction she'd find her hotel.

"No more talk about religion. I promise."

"I just want to go home," she murmured. She meant it too. Home to Wisconsin. This vacation had lost its glow.

"Okay. Well, then let me get you a cab."

She folded her arms in front of her and turned away from Mike. Not only did she feel frightened at the moment, she felt downright stupid. Where did she think she was going in a strange foreign city, and with no money, in the middle of the night? Moreover, Mike had no power over her. She didn't have to be afraid of him.

Her common sense began to return.

"I think I'm just reacting to everything that's happened tonight," she muttered, more to herself than to him. "Like posttraumatic stress or something."

"I'm sure you are. C'mon," he said gently, taking hold of her elbow and leading her back to the coffeehouse. "I'll call that cab."

Unable to do much else, Risa allowed him to guide her back into the coffeehouse.

four

Mike watched Risa's cab drive away and marveled at the sudden change in her mood. He tried not to take it personally, but he couldn't seem to help it. He told himself it was God she reacted to, not him; and being in the ministry, Mike thought he should be used to the cold-shoulder routine by now.

He sighed, wishing Risa hadn't refused his offer to see her safely back to the hotel. He would have felt better if he'd been able to accompany her.

Rubbing the back of his neck, he realized how exhausted he felt. It'd been a long day, and he was in for another of the same tomorrow. If he'd been smart, he would have gone straight back to his own hotel after leaving the hospital. However, the truth was, he hadn't wanted to say good night to Risa. His attraction to her was something he really couldn't fathom, and he certainly hadn't dwelled upon it these past weeks. He'd done his best to give the matter over to the Lord.

And then tonight. . .

Imagine running into her here in Palermo! Mike couldn't deny the fact that it had been a miracle. Even though he'd refrained from calling her during the past month, he'd been wondering how she was faring just the same. Tonight, it seemed God had allowed him to see where Risa was spiritually, so he'd know how to pray. He'd gotten the impression that she was standing at the crossroads, facing a decision that would impact her eternity. He was helpless, powerless, to persuade her to choose Christ, but he could pray. And pray he would!

Mike turned on his heel and reentered the coffeehouse, where he summoned another cab. While he waited, he made small talk with Anthony and Maria, who were closing up shop for the night. He felt relieved that his friends didn't inquire about Risa's hasty departure. He didn't know Italian well enough for long explanations. Instead, they asked more questions about family in America, and Mike did his best to reply.

Minutes later, the taxi arrived. Since the three of them had previously exchanged E-mail addresses and promised to keep in touch, Mike bid the married couple good-bye and left.

During the ride home in the darkened cab, it was all he could do to stay awake. Reaching the hotel, he paid the driver, then headed inside and up to the room he shared with John Schmidt, the father of one of the youth group girls. John had come along on the mission trip to help chaperone. He'd also aided Mike and had taken off after the thugs who attacked Risa and her friend Kari.

"How are those two women?" John asked as Mike entered the hotel room. "Okay, I hope."

"Yeah, they're okay. Kari's got a black eye and probably a concussion, but she'll be released from the hospital tomorrow. Risa's fine physically. Just a bit shaken." Mike glanced at his roommate, a large man who stood over six feet tall and was somewhere in his early fifties. John's hair was dusty gray, but his face still radiated a boyish exuberance that was contagious. He had helped make this mission trip a lot of fun.

"It was good of you to stay at the hospital for awhile," John said with a yawn. "It's always nice to see a familiar face when you're in a situation like those ladies were in. I'm sure they appreciated your comfort and support."

Mike just smiled, thinking his motives were more along the lines of selfishness than a sense of duty. Even so, he'd helped Risa by paying for her cab ride back to her hotel, if nothing else.

He prepared for bed, pulling on a pair of gym shorts and a T-shirt. Next, he strode to the bathroom and brushed his teeth.

"The kids are excited about touring the marionette

museum tomorrow," John said when Mike reentered the room. He watched the older man crawl into one of the two double beds.

Mike grinned. "Yeah, that'll be fun."

"But the kids said they'd like to go to the hospital first and sing for some of the patients. What do you think?"

"That's a great idea. Did they come up with it on their own?"

"Sure did."

Mike slipped underneath his own bedcovers, feeling impressed by the sensitivity of the teens. "How's Mary Beth doing?"

"Oh, fine. She's as chatty as ever and seems to be keeping up with the others. I think she's getting past her insecurities and becoming burdened for unbelievers. This trip has been a real blessing for her in that respect."

"God is good," Mike replied.

Reaching over to his far left, he switched off the light that was posted above the headboard. He said quick prayers for his family, the youth group, Kari, Risa, and Mary Beth. For the first time he realized that the latter two females had a lot in common. For starters, they were products of broken homes, and, although Mike didn't know too much more about Risa's past, he did know that Mary Beth had it tough. Her stepmother was addicted to cocaine, and her dad worked long hours. Mary Beth had used drugs, and last year, at the tender age of fourteen, she'd attempted suicide. John's daughter Tracy had heard about the near-tragedy in school and went to visit Mary Beth in the hospital. A friendship ensued, and soon Mary Beth was attending church. Mike didn't have to think twice about allowing the young lady to come along on this trip, especially since John had unofficially adopted her, and he and Tracy were going. Mike sensed that Mary Beth had the potential to serve God; however, her tumultuous home life was a hindrance. Her insecurities and self-consciousness hung in a delicate balance, and when the discouragement hit, Mary

Beth didn't cope with it well. Even so, God could overcome all obstacles.

Mike yawned before contemplating all the exciting things the Lord was doing, and suddenly he looked forward to the morning.

≥∙

Risa awoke to the sound of raindrops splashing against the hotel's windows and onto the patio's tin roof. Throwing off her bedcovers, she padded to the sliding glass doors, pulled back the draperies, and peered out at the gloomy morning. It seemed somehow to match her mood, and Risa was tempted to crawl back into bed until she remembered Kari at the hospital, waiting for her. Gathering her resolve, she headed for the bathroom and showered. Afterward, she dressed quickly, thinking her friend would be ready to leave the hospital soon. Brushing her hair, Risa pulled it back and stayed it with a plastic clip. Then, tucking some money into her jeans pocket, she left the hotel room.

In the lobby she summoned a cab, and while she waited out front for its arrival, she noticed a rainbow high in the sky, as the rain dissipated and the sun began to work its way through the dark clouds. Glancing about the street, she wondered if anyone else saw it, but those passing by seemed oblivious to the colorful display arching across the heavens.

What does it mean? she wondered. Ever since Risa was a little girl, she had equated weather with God's moods. When it rained, He was sad. The thunder and lightning meant He was angry. The snow and cold of Wisconsin winters meant God was smiling down on Florida for the season and had turned His back on the northern regions.

Risa smiled. How silly. God didn't really care what was going on down here. . .did He? As long as people tried to do the best they could, wasn't that okay with God?

The taxicab pulled up to the curb and honked to get Risa's attention. Giving herself a mental shake, she climbed into the backseat of the car and did her best to explain her destination to the driver. He was a burly fellow with long, slick black hair tied back in a ponytail. His brown eyes seemed to express his understanding about where she wanted to go. Nevertheless, the ride to the hospital proved long, hot, and humid, and the traffic in Palermo seemed worse than usual. But an hour later, Risa arrived at the hospital. It took a bit more time to locate Kari's room, but at last she stood at her friend's bedside.

"You should have heard the kids who came to sing for me this morning," Kari said. Her left eye looked even more swollen than it had last night, and the surrounding bruise had grown an ugly dark purple. "They were terrific. Pastor Mike brought them around. Nice guy, that pastor."

"Yeah, I suppose," Risa replied, sitting down in the chair next to the bed. How could she deny it? Mike had helped her out last night and paid her way home. "But I've never known a mean clergyman," she added. "They're supposed to be nice. It's their job."

"You sound kinda defensive. What's up, Ris?"

"Nothing's up." She looked at the pamphlet in her friend's hand and recognized that it was identical to the one Wren had given her long ago. "I see the kids who were here gave you more than a song."

Kari looked down at the gospel tract. "Yeah. I was reading it when you walked in."

"Well, forget it. It's just propaganda."

"Hmm, I thought just the opposite," Kari replied with a thoughtful expression. "This kinda makes sense, and it's nothing different from what I was taught in Sunday school." She opened the leaflet and began to read. "Jesus died, was buried, and rose the third day." She looked at Risa. "You believe that, right? I do. I mean, I always try to go to church on Easter Sunday."

"Yeah, me too." Risa had heard those three truths proclaimed from pulpits all her life. But what did it have to do with her?

Kari began to read again, and it was all Risa could do to sit still and listen. However, she determined that she wasn't going to run away anymore. She could believe what she wanted regardless of what born-again Christians said. After all, it was the same God.

"Jesus died for sinners and the Bible says 'all have sinned and come short of the glory of God.' In other words," Kari read, "Jesus died for you." She glanced up, her one eye puffy and black and blue. "We believe that much, right?"

"I guess so."

"I know I've sinned," Kari muttered.

Risa smirked. "Who hasn't?" And then, like pesky unwanted mice, a dozen episodes that would likely be deemed "sin" scampered across her memory. But she didn't want to think about them. She glanced toward the door, wondering if she should find the cafeteria and buy something to eat.

Kari continued to read the tract. "As God's only begotten Son, Jesus led a sinless life. He became the Lamb of God, the spotless lamb, the perfect sacrifice for our sins."

"Kari, enough already. When are you getting out of this joint?"

"I don't know. Whenever Dr. Cappella decides to spring me, I guess." She looked back down at the pamphlet in her hands. "We're sinners deserving of eternal punishment, which is death and hell. But Jesus died in our place so we could live forever with Him in heaven. Who but God could endure the wrath of God? Only Christ, and He said, 'I am the way and the truth and the life. No one comes to the Father except through me.' Accept the Lord Jesus as your personal Savior today." Kari swung her gaze upward. "Okay, Jesus, I accept you."

Risa rolled her eyes and shook her head. "It's not that easy."

"But this pamphlet says to accept Jesus and I do."

Risa shrugged. "Whatever. I'm no expert. It just seems too. . .too simple."

This time Kari shrugged. "Maybe it is." She paused, giving the tract a long, pensive stare. "But, you know? I've got this strange sensation—it's like a deep peace inside of me—that wasn't there before. I think it's God."

"You're beginning to worry me, Kari. I think there's been some brain damage."

She appeared suddenly embarrassed. "Oh, fine. Think what you want."

At that moment Dr. Cappella entered the room. He wore dark blue casual pants and a white lab coat over a blue-and-white-striped dress shirt. "Good afternoon," he said with a grin. "How are the two American women faring on this lovely day?"

Risa smiled at the stout but handsome physician. "I'm great. But the million-dollar question is, how's your patient?"

He winced as he looked at Kari, obviously taking in her swollen eye. "Perhaps we should nickname her Bruiser."

"Yeah, well, that's what they call me at home," she quipped with another laugh.

Smiling, the doctor lifted Kari's chart and began making notes. "The X-ray looked okay. I think you'll be fine, so we will release you. But don't overdo it."

"Don't worry. I'm not going out in public looking like this!"

Risa chuckled softly at her friend's reply, and the doctor's grin broadened. Then, after penning some instructions, he handed Kari her discharge papers. With that, he wished them both the best and left the room.

"Nice guy," Kari said. "Too bad he's married. All the good ones are taken, you know?"

"Yep," Risa stated on a flat note as thoughts of Wren flitted across her mind. She mentally shook herself and stood. "Well, c'mon. Get up and dress so we can ditch this place and enjoy the rest of our vacation." She sighed before adding, "Even if we have to spend it in our hotel room."

five

By the time Risa and Kari returned to their hotel room, the midafternoon sun was streaming through the glass patio doors.

"Want to sit outside awhile? There's a nice breeze coming in off the sea."

Kari nodded her bruised head. "Sounds good."

Together they made their way onto the porch that over-looked a bustling street. Each selected a colorful padded lawn chair and sat down. Below them, Risa could hear men shout to one another amid the droning of the afternoon traffic. Despite the noise, however, the sun felt warm and comforting—like a heating blanket—and she couldn't deny the correlation between sunshine and happiness, rain and depression.

She glanced over at Kari. "Ever wonder why the weather affects our moods?"

"I think it's something to do with the barometer."

And not with God, Risa added silently. Then she mentally shoved the thought aside. "It turned out to be a nice day."

"Yeah, you'd never guess it was raining this morning."

Risa agreed before settling back and resting her legs on the wrought iron patio rail.

"I phoned my mother from the hospital to let her know what happened. She was mad at me for calling collect."

Risa didn't have a reply. . .a polite one, anyway. She knew Kari and her mother's relationship was strained, at best. Kari wasn't close to any of her family members, and they always balked when she asked them to help care for two-year-old Jodi.

"So, what did you end up doing last night after you left the hospital?" Kari asked. "How did you get back here without your purse or money?"

41

"Mike helped me out. We stopped for coffee first."

"A date with a pastor, eh?"

Risa rolled her eyes. "Yeah, right. Some date. Like I said before, Mike's looking for another convert. That's it."

Kari sighed. "I guess you'd know. But I don't see what the big deal is. I mean, it's not like Mike believes some wacky theology. It's all Bible stuff."

Risa shifted her gaze to Kari, thinking she sounded a whole lot different now than she had back in the mall when they decided to make this trip. "Bible or not, pastors are boring, remember?"

"I remember. . .but I think I'm changing my mind about what's fun and exciting. Look what happened to us last night."

In spite of herself, Risa couldn't argue the point.

She stared out over the balcony at some people passing by. Her insides were still all churned up over the mugging incident and the events that followed.

"I hope I haven't ruined your vacation by not being able to go out."

Risa looked at Kari. "Not a chance. It's hardly your fault we got robbed. And for your information, I'm not in the least disappointed. It'll be nice to sit around tonight. I need some relaxation time. We've been on the go since we arrived in Italy."

"True." Kari gave her a small smile. "Okay, tell you what. . .we'll order dinner delivered to our room and watch an Italian movie and try to figure out the plot."

"Sounds like a plan," Risa said with a chuckle. She stood. "I want a cola. Maybe it'll settle my stomach. How 'bout you?"

"Sure."

Pivoting, Risa reentered the room and strode to the other side, where she opened the outer door. She traipsed down the hallway, and at its far end she pulled some money from her jeans pocket and purchased two sodas from the vending machine. Carrying a can in each hand, she walked back to the room.

"Tired of sitting outside?" she asked Kari, who stood near one of the two beds.

"I feel kind of weird. . .and suddenly my head is killing me. It's like something exploded in my brain."

"You look a bit pale," Risa said, noting her friend's ashen face. "Maybe you'd better lie down."

Kari readily complied.

Setting the cans of pop on the desk, Risa went to the bathroom and soaked a washcloth with cold water. Maybe Kari was getting a migraine or something. "Here, try this," she said, placing the cool, damp cloth on her friend's forehead.

Kari didn't reply.

"Kari?" Risa thought it strange that she'd fallen asleep so quickly. But perhaps she'd had some sort of pain medication earlier at the hospital.

Moving toward the desk, Risa grabbed her cola, flipped open the top, and took a long drink. Then she sat down in the nearby chair and scrutinized her friend, deciding she didn't look good. In fact, she looked. . .

"Kari!" Was she even breathing?

Risa jumped up and ran to her. With a hand on the woman's shoulder, she gave her several mild shakes.

No response.

Putting her ear to Kari's chest, Risa listened, but couldn't hear a heartbeat.

"This can't be happening," she muttered, bolting toward the phone. She dialed the main desk, and three rings later a male attendant answered.

"Allo."

"I need an ambulance!" Risa cried.

"Ambulanza?"

"Si. Subito. . .right away."

"Si, si," the clerk replied. He double-checked the room number.

"Correct. Room 204."

Risa dropped the receiver into its holder and sat down beside Kari. She reached for her hand. It felt cold, lifeless.

"No, no," she repeated, squeezing her eyes shut against the horror. "This can't be happening!"

≥∘

Mike felt proud of the kids as he listened to their testimonies about how they were able to share the gospel while on this mission trip. As the four adults and eight teens sat together on a pier, some of the kids with their bare feet dangling into the frothy sea waves, they took turns sharing their experiences over the past several days. Mike had to admit that he was impressed by the deep sensitivity of the teenagers. There was no doubt about their commitment to see lost souls saved.

"The Lord prompted me to give a tract to that lady in the hospital," Mary Beth Canfield said. "It was one from church that I had in my pocket. I could tell that woman needed Jesus. I could see it in her eyes, and I've been praying for her all afternoon."

Mike gave the girl a warm smile. "I've been praying too."

"What do you mean you could 'see it in her eyes'?" one of the boys asked. "Her eyes were pretty messed up—one of them, anyhow."

Mike couldn't stifle the grin that tugged at the corners of his mouth.

"Well, I saw it, okay?" Mary Beth said with an impatient toss of her light brown hair. "She had that. . .look. I see it on my mom sometimes too. It's sorta like they know how it feels to be kicked around the block a few times, so it shows on their faces."

No one uttered another word for several long moments.

"You know," Mike began, "there's a world full of broken-hearted people out there who God wants us to reach. He puts them in our path at the grocery store, at restaurants. . . ."

"On airplanes," Tim Johnson interjected. He'd already shared the story about how he'd led an elderly woman to

Christ during the flight to Italy.

Mike grinned. "That's right. And my point is this: Wherever we go, we have to believe that it's no accident or coincidence when our paths cross with unbelievers." He couldn't help but think of Risa and her friend as he spoke. "As Christians, we know the truth and we have a responsibility to share it. That's what this mission trip is all about, right?"

The group nodded.

"Can we eat now, Preacher?" Allen Tabors asked, wearing a smirk. "I'm starving."

The teenage boys agreed in hearty unison, while Leslie Owens, another adult sponsor, gave Allen a peeved glance.

"Can't you think of anything besides food?" she asked.

"I'm in Italy," he replied, raking his long fingers through his sandy blond hair. "Not thinking about food here is like not getting thirsty on an ocean cruise."

Everyone laughed.

Mike stood. "I'm hungry too. Let's go."

"Excuse me, Pastor," Leslie said. She was a widow who had lost her husband in a skiing accident. The tragedy had occurred before Mike was hired at Bay Community Church, but he'd learned the details from Kevin and from Leslie too. "Before we go to the restaurant, I need to stop back at the hotel."

"Sure thing," Mike answered. He turned and led the way down the street. Arriving minutes later, the teens scrambled for seats in the well-decorated lobby. Just as soon as they'd gotten comfortable, the girls began whispering and giggling about some silly thing that Mike couldn't understand—even after questioning all four of them.

"Don't worry about it," John assured him. "Girls just do this sometimes."

Mike figured the man ought to know.

"Tracy and her friends sound like magpies when they're together. Can't even tell who's listening, so I sure don't."

Mike chuckled.

"My wife says it's a sign that they're normal teenage girls."

"That's good. . .I guess. But it makes me feel sorry for Leslie, having to share a room with them."

"Are you kidding? Tracy tells me she lays down the law with those girls. You don't have to worry about Leslie." He gave Mike an elbow. "The widow probably needs a man to soften her up, don't you think?"

Mike smiled patiently. "I wouldn't know." And he didn't feel interested enough to explore the possibility, either, although he did appreciate Leslie volunteering to chaperone the girls on this trip.

"Pastor Mike?"

He looked across the lobby and watched Craig Drummond, a redheaded, freckle-faced kid and one of the four boys on the mission team, coming toward him.

"The dude behind the desk told me to give this to you. . .at least, that's what I think he told me to do."

Mike watched Craig peer over his shoulder and then saw the clerk nod approvingly.

"Yeah, I guess I understood him."

He handed Mike a piece of paper on which a message in Italian had been penned. "Oh, great," he muttered. "I can't read a single word. . . . No, wait. . .maybe I can."

He made out the name *Cappella* and guessed it was Joe who had called. He'd also left his number.

"I'm going to check this out," Mike told John. "Be right back."

"No problem. You won't miss much. The girls'll still be giggling, I'm sure."

Craig scrunched up his face into a disgusted frown and Mike laughed as he walked to the courtesy phone on the wall and placed the call. After being transferred, he heard Joe's voice on the other end of the line.

"Can you come to the hospital right away?"

"Well, um. . ." He looked back at the group of teens, Allen

Tabors, John Schmidt, and now Leslie Owens. They were waiting for him. But they had all enjoyed the hospital ministry this morning and probably wouldn't mind going back. "We could be there after supper."

"Not 'we,' Mike. You. And it's important."

Mike frowned. "What's up?"

"Risa asked me to call you. Her friend Kari developed a subdural hematoma. But nothing showed up on the X-ray."

"What does that mean?"

A pause. "She's dead, Mike. She died this afternoon."

He stood there, paralyzed from the news, and stared blindly at the grandfather clock standing near the hotel's front entrance.

"Naturally, Risa is quite upset."

"I'm on my way."

"Thanks."

Still somewhat dazed, Mike hung up the phone and walked over to the group. He explained the situation. "Go ahead and have dinner without me," he added.

"Okay, but we'll be praying," John promised.

"Thanks."

Mike turned and made his way for the door.

"I hope that lady read the tract I gave her," he heard Mary Beth say as he exited the hotel.

six

Mike found Risa in what the hospital called its "Quiet Center." Located across from the chapel, it offered a place of solace where families could wait for word on their loved ones and where doctors could confer with them about decisions that needed to be made.

"Risa?"

Mike approached her with quiet steps, Joe Cappella right on his heels. She turned from the window, her eyes puffy, and Mike's heart ached for her.

"I can't believe she's dead," Risa said. She swallowed hard, and Mike could tell she fought against a fresh onset of tears. "Just twenty-four hours ago, Kari and I were having a blast. Now she's. . .gone."

Mike sent up an arrow of a prayer, asking for wisdom, a word fitly spoken.

"I told Risa I'd give her something to help her sleep tonight," Joe explained. "But she refused any medication."

She returned her gaze to the window.

"What about Kari's family?" Mike asked in hushed tones. "Have they been notified?"

"Yes, I phoned them," Joe replied.

Risa put her face in her hands. "I can't believe she's dead. Why? I don't understand why this happened."

Mike stepped forward and put his hand on her shoulder.

"What's going to happen to Jodi now?" she sobbed.

She swung around and Mike stepped back, noticing the tears leaking from the corners of her hazel eyes.

She sniffed. "None of Kari's family will want custody, I know that much, and Jodi's father is a—well, I won't say it in front of you, a pastor."

Once more she turned her back on him and Joe.

"Risa, let me give you something to help you sleep tonight," the doctor offered again. "The pain of your loss will still be there tomorrow, but at least you'll be clear-headed after a good night's rest."

Mike thought that made sense. "Risa? Why don't you let Joe give you some medicine?"

She did a one-eighty and stared at him with bleary eyes. "Because I don't want to go back to the hotel room," she said, her voice strained. "Not tonight. Not ever!"

"Hey, look, I can understand that." Mike turned to Joe. "She can come home with me."

The moment the words were out of his mouth, Mike realized his blunder. He felt his face reddening from embarrassment, and the shocked look on Risa's face didn't help matters.

"I, um, didn't mean that the way it sounded," he said lamely. "What I meant to say is that our mission team has three hotel rooms, and I'm sure the ladies can accommodate you, Risa." He cleared his throat.

Joe grinned. "I stay out of this kind of stuff."

A slow smile spread across Risa's face, and then she burst out laughing. She laughed so hard, she had to sit down. "Oh, that was precious, Mike," she said. But then, a heartbeat later, the gloom obviously descended again. "Kari would have hooted over that one."

With that she put her head into her lap and began sobbing all over again.

A jolt of concern coursed through Mike's being. He looked at Joe.

"It's the shock that's causing her strange reaction," he explained, as if divining his thoughts. "I'll be right back. I'm going to get that medicine."

Hunkering beside Risa's chair, Mike set his hand on the base of her neck. "I know it hurts," he whispered.

"It h–hurts so bad," she cried.

"I know, I know." Mike felt like weeping himself.

"It happened so fast." Risa raised her head and met his gaze. "One minute we were sitting on the patio talking, and the next minute, she was dead."

Mike pursed his lips and nodded sympathetically.

"I don't understand," Risa sobbed. "Why? Why did this happen?"

"I wish I knew the perfect answer to that question. It's been asked of me many times."

"Is God punishing me?" she asked softly, her chin quivering.

Mike gave her a little smile. "I don't think God works that way. A death like this is a hard thing to understand, and I won't pretend to have all the answers. But one thing I do know, Risa, is that God loves you very much and He wants the best for you."

"How is this the best? Kari's dead. Dead!"

"I don't know." Mike shook his head. He could think of at least ten sermons that he'd preached on the subject of death—why it happens and how it was never God's ideal for mankind—but he sensed Risa wouldn't want to hear any of them right now.

She sat back, and Mike retracted his arm. "Well, if you born-agains are right, then I think Kari's in heaven."

"What do you mean?"

Risa swallowed convulsively, as if trying to rein in her emotions. "Kari read that leaflet thing you and your church group left with her this morning. She said she accepted Jesus, but I didn't think it was that easy." Risa paused. "Is it?"

Mike smiled. "Yes, it sure is. The plan of salvation is so simple, a child can understand it. In fact, that's how we're to come to God, with hearts like children."

"So is Kari in heaven?"

"If she accepted Christ as her Savior, she is. We can know that for certain because the Bible says so."

"Does it?" Risa seemed comforted to hear that.

"It's written that to be absent from the body is to be present with the Lord. Unfortunately, some will meet Him as the judge who will administer eternal punishment to lost sinners. But others will meet Him as their loving God, and He'll welcome them with open arms. It just depends on us."

"Don't try to scare me, Mike, or force me to make a decision I'm not ready to make."

He shook his head. "I don't mean to be pushy. Honest. But the reason I chose my profession is because I believe the Bible. A Scripture that applies here is 2 Corinthians 5:11. I chose it as my life's verse: 'Knowing, therefore, the terror of the Lord, we persuade men.'

"You see, Risa," he continued, "death will be a frightening thing for people who refuse to accept Christ, but it will be a blessed homecoming for those who were miraculously saved by grace."

Risa opened her mouth in what Mike felt sure would be a rebuttal, but then Joe Cappella entered the room. She took one glance at the syringe in his hand and balked. "Oh no, you're not sticking me with any needles."

"Oh, yes I am," Joe countered. "But it won't hurt."

Mike had to chuckle at Risa's surprised expression. She obviously hadn't expected an argument. Fortunately, Joe made quick work of administering the injection before she could further any debate.

"You lied," she told him, rubbing her upper arm. "It did too hurt."

Joe donned a rather rakish grin. "Sorry."

"Doctors and pastors," she said on a disgusted note as she rose from her chair. "I've had enough of both of you." She took several strides toward the door, but then whirled around. "Are you taking me home, Mike, or what?"

In reply, he saluted. Then, grinning, he faced Joe. "Good to see you again," he said as they clasped hands in a parting shake. "Thanks for everything."

"You bet. Drop me a line sometime."

Mike nodded before following Risa out of the Quiet Center.

છ

"I think she's waking up, Mrs. Owens," Risa heard a female voice say; the voice sounded young.

Peeling open one eyelid, Risa stared up at the girl leaning over her. Light brown hair framed the worried blue eyes that looked back.

"Who are you?" Risa asked. She hoisted herself onto an elbow and quickly took in her surroundings. "Where am I?"

"You're at Hotel Bellavista," another woman replied in a matter-of-fact tone, "and you're among friends. I'm Leslie Owens, and this is Mary Beth Canfield."

"Nice to meet you," Risa said a bit skeptically. She remembered getting into the cab with Mike, but after that, everything was a blur. Glancing down at her attire, she realized she wore nothing but an oversized T-shirt. "Where are my clothes?"

"They're over here," Mary Beth told her, pointing to where her jeans, blouse, and undergarments had been slung over the back of a chair. "We helped you into something more comfy to sleep in, except. . ." She looked at the other woman. "Except Mrs. Owens and I didn't have a clean nightie because we're at the end of our trip, so Pastor Mike donated one of his shirts. He said it was washed."

I slept in one of Mike's shirts? Risa felt uncomfortable about that, but didn't quite know why. Add to it the rest of her tumultuous emotions, and she figured her mind was one fine mess.

"This has got to be a bad dream," she said, falling back against the pillows. The impact of Kari's death yesterday suddenly bore down on her like a crushing weight, and she squeezed her eyes closed against the pain. "Make that a nightmare. This is definitely a nightmare."

"I'm really sorry about your friend," Mary Beth said, lowering herself onto the edge of the bed. "But I'm rejoicing because Pastor Mike said she'd accepted the Lord before she died."

Risa opened her eyes and considered the girl, her smile, the look of gladness in her eyes. How could she be rejoicing at a time like this? Risa just didn't get it—and she didn't understand these people.

"I've got to get out of here," she said, tossing off the bedcovers and clambering to her feet. The room swayed, and she felt sick to her stomach. "Oh, my head. . ."

Leslie Owens walked purposely to her side and took her elbow. "It's probably the effects of the medicine."

"Probably," Risa agreed.

"Why don't you crawl back into bed for a bit," the woman suggested. "Mary Beth will fetch you a cup of coffee, and there's a continental breakfast in the lobby. Oh, and Mary Beth, get a bagel or something for Miss Vitalis."

"Yes, Ma'am."

The teenager was out the door before Risa could utter a single protest.

Turning her head, Risa looked at Leslie, almost studying her in that brief few moments, and she decided the woman was pretty, but in a plain sort of way. She was tall, perhaps Mike's height, except she was as thin as a reed, which made her seem even taller. Silky golden hair framed her delicate features and creamy complexion. Her lips were thin but a natural pink, and her eyes were as blue as cornflowers.

"I know this will sound very trite," Leslie said with an earnest expression, "but everything will be all right. You'll see. Your friend's death has come as no surprise to God. He is still on His thrown, ruling the universe."

"It doesn't sound trite. It sounds. . .confusing," Risa declared, lowering herself back into bed.

"Yes, I imagine it does. It's very hard to make sense out of a loved one's death. I know. God took my husband home a few years ago. I was a widow at the age of thirty. And don't be fooled into thinking that just because I'm a Christian, I can handle anything and everything that comes my way. I'm afraid I managed things very badly." She sat down on the opposite bed. "I felt bewildered, angry with God, betrayed by Him," she stated thoughtfully. "But through those stormy months following Hal's death, the Lord proved His promises to me over and over again. His promises were like. . .like my rainbow in the rain."

At the word "rainbow," something stirred inside Risa and she recalled yesterday morning's colorful arch that spanned the heavens. It seemed as though it had been painted in the sky just for her.

But of course, it hadn't been.

There were scientific reasons for rainbows, and they had nothing to do with God.

Risa swallowed hard. "I feel like I'm going nuts." She put her head in her hands. "Or maybe the world's gone crazy."

"The world has always been crazy," Leslie replied tartly. "And you're thinking too hard at a very stressful time. Just relax and trust God, Miss Vitalis. Give Him everything, your confusion, your pain. . . ."

"But don't I have to give Him my soul first?" Risa retorted.

"Well, of course. . .but who else would you want to give it to?"

Risa mentally searched for a comeback; however, the truth of the matter was, the question had left her speechless.

Who else. . . ? Duh! There *was* no one else. She sure didn't want the devil to have her soul! Was that the decision Mike wanted her to make? Why didn't he just say so? It was kind of a no-brainer. Maybe salvation was as easy as Kari thought and Mike had said.

Okay, God, Risa prayed, *if it's mine to give, You've got my soul. It's Yours.* She lay back down and pulled the covers up to her chin, marveling at the sudden calm wafting over her.

seven

Mary Beth returned with a tray containing enough food for ten people. Feeling as though she could eat something now, Risa selected a large blueberry muffin from the assortment of goodies and gratefully accepted a cup of black coffee.

"Are your things packed, Mary Beth?" Leslie asked the girl who had seated herself on the edge of Risa's bed.

"Yes, Ma'am."

After an approving nod, Leslie looked at Risa. "We fly home this afternoon. What day are you scheduled to leave?"

"Friday, but. . ." Risa thought it over. "I really want to go home now."

"Maybe there's room on our flight," Mary Beth suggested. "What airline are you traveling on?"

Risa told her.

"Oh." Mary Beth's expression fell. "We're on a different one."

For lack of a better reply, Risa shrugged.

"Won't it cost a lot of money to reschedule?" Leslie asked. "Airline tickets are usually nonrefundable, aren't they?"

"I don't even care," Risa replied. "I just want to get out of here and go home."

"I don't blame you," Leslie said, folding some clothes and tucking them into her suitcase.

Risa chewed her muffin and watched the other woman busily packing for her trip home. She took a sip of coffee, dreading her return to the hotel. She supposed she would have to gather Kari's things and bring them home with her, and she tried not to think about Kari's body and how it would be transported back to the United States. Instead, Risa

55

chose to assume the hospital and Kari's family had worked out the details.

A wave of nausea forced Risa to abandon the rest of her muffin as she thought about little Jodi. Most likely the little girl would be bounced between her father's and grandmother's homes. Risa decided then and there to let Kari's family know she was willing to help any way she could.

Shaking off her reverie, she noticed that Mary Beth was staring at her.

"I like your hair," the girl said.

Risa groaned and self-consciously combed her fingers through her thick curls. "It probably needs a good brushing."

"Do you get a perm or is it naturally curly?"

"It's naturally a mess," Risa said with a laugh. "I'd love to have straight hair like yours."

Mary Beth smiled and flipped several strands of her light brown hair over her shoulder. "I'd love to have curls like yours."

Risa grinned.

"Let's be thankful for what God's given us, Ladies," Leslie admonished in a gentle tone. She folded her robe and set it in her suitcase.

Risa noticed that Leslie had dressed and now wore a navy blue skirt and plain white blouse. Her blond hair had been pulled back into a severe knot—a no-nonsense hairdo and outfit for a no-nonsense kind of woman.

Glancing at Mary Beth again, Risa gave her a helpless shrug. "I s'pose I'd better get my clothes on. I'm sure Mike wants his shirt back."

"You can leave it with me," Leslie said. "I'll make certain he gets it."

"Okay, sure." Risa crawled from beneath the bedcovers, feeling suddenly out of place, awkward. Maybe Leslie had a lot to accomplish before leaving this afternoon. Maybe she felt stressed. There was something in her demeanor that made Risa think so, although one wouldn't guess that by the sound of Leslie's voice, still soft-spoken and controlled.

Risa grabbed her clothes and walked into the bathroom. Closing the door, she heard Leslie giving Mary Beth a list of tasks. *Maybe the woman has a military background*, Risa thought as she pulled on her jeans.

Once dressed, Risa looked in the mirror and did her best to tame her unruly mane. Finally, she gave up. Leaving the bathroom, she found her shoes and slipped them on. As she handed Mike's shirt to Leslie, a knock sounded at the door. Mary Beth rushed to answer it.

"Hi, Pastor Mike."

"Good morning. Everyone up and moving?"

"Yep."

Mary Beth opened the door wider, and Mike took a few steps into the room. "Everybody okay?"

Risa glanced in his direction, sensing he meant her. Mike was looking right at her.

"I'm okay," she replied.

"We're fine. Just about all packed," Leslie added.

"Good." Mike narrowed his gaze, obviously recognizing the red garment in Leslie's possession. "Is that my shirt?"

"Oh, um, yes," she stammered. "Here."

Leslie thrust it at Mike, her face aflame with embarrassment, and Risa was hard pressed to contain her mirth. The woman acted like she'd been clutching his BVDs or something. Risa decided that if Kari were here, she'd have died laughing at the situation.

It's just too bad she died for real, Risa thought. It was still so hard to believe that Kari truly was gone.

A knot of despair lodged in her chest.

"What are your plans, Risa?"

She glanced at Mike, who flung the shirt over his shoulder. He either hadn't noticed Leslie's chagrin or else he had chosen to ignore it.

She swallowed a lump of remorse. "I want to go home."

"I figured as much. If you want, we can stop at your hotel so you can collect your luggage, and then we'll all head to the airport together."

"Yeah!" Mary Beth said, appearing energized by the idea. "You won't have to be alone if you're with us. I know what it's like to be sad and by yourself."

Risa felt suddenly very curious. What kind of grief could this young girl have experienced that would cause her to understand the kind of anguish in Risa's heart? She would have asked, but Leslie cut in.

"There's no guarantee that you'll leave Sicily today," she warned. "Every departing flight might be booked."

"True. But at least I'll be at the airport ready to go. I don't care if the airline puts me on standby for the next twenty-four hours."

"Well, let's pray that doesn't happen," Mike said. "God is able to work out a flight schedule."

Risa managed a polite smile. "We'll see, won't we?"

ಶ

As it happened, God not only worked out Risa's itinerary, He made it so she didn't have to pay one extra dime for the change. When the supervisor of the airline heard about the robbery and Kari's resulting death, he pulled strings and obtained a first-class seat for Risa all the way to O'Hare in Chicago. From there, she could drive Kari's car back to Milwaukee, since they had parked it in one of the airport's long-term lots.

"You sure you don't want something to eat?" Mike asked as he, Risa, and the others sat in a food court somewhere between their two separate boarding gates.

She looked at the thick slab of greasy pizza he'd purchased and felt queasy. "No, thanks. I'm really not very hungry."

Mary Beth was sitting on Risa's other side. "Do you wear makeup?" she asked.

"Yes, but I don't have any on today, and I'm sure I look a fright."

"No way," the girl disagreed. "I think you look good. . . doesn't she, Pastor Mike?"

"I think Risa always looks good." He took a bite of his pizza.

"Yeah, right." Grinning, she watched him lift his paper napkin to wipe his mouth. Not only was he polite, but Risa noticed that Mike always displayed a tidy appearance. Today was no exception. From his khaki trousers and a navy blue and beige-collared T-shirt to his neatly parted dark brown hair, he seemed a fitting role model for the teens on this mission trip.

She, in contrast, felt bedraggled at best. Wearing her clothes from yesterday and not having taken a shower this morning, her hair wild and frizzy, Risa imagined she looked like a homeless person on a day when all the shelters were full. She felt certain she wasn't much of an example to Mike's church group, especially Mary Beth, who had practically fastened herself to Risa's side.

"So what kind of makeup do you wear?"

"Well, I. . ." Risa caught a glance of Leslie standing in a food line talking with one of the teenaged girls. Risa guessed the willowy blond didn't wear a stitch of makeup, not that she needed to. She had a natural beauty about her. On the other hand, a soft shade of eye shadow, a hint of blush. . .and if she let her hair down, she probably wouldn't look so prissy.

Mary Beth nudged her. "Look at the lipstick I bought when Tracy and I went shopping." She produced a shiny pink tube from the zipper pouch of her backpack. "See? It has sparkles in it. I think it's neat."

Risa inspected the color, Very Berry, with minuscule glitter. Next, she tested it on the top of her hand. Smiling, she gave it back to Mary Beth. "I like that. Where did you get it? My niece would love one of those."

"At the mall in a boutique that's right next to the big department store."

"I'll have to look for it."

"Pastor?" Leslie called from her place in line. "I think half our team needs some direction." She pointed down the food court, where four sixteen-year-old boys were playing keep-away with one of the teen girls' purses. As they tossed it back and forth, the two girls were squealing and shouting at the boys to stop.

Mike nodded and stood. "I just hate it when they act like teenagers," he muttered facetiously.

Risa couldn't help a smile before glancing at her watch. Her plane would depart in an hour. She'd be boarding soon.

"Know what?" Mary Beth said, leaning over conspiratorially, "I think Mrs. Owens has it bad for Pastor Mike."

"Has it bad. . .as in having a crush on him?"

"Yep."

"Hmm. . ." Risa found that tidbit interesting. "And does Pastor Mike have it bad for her?"

"Nope."

Risa turned to the girl. "How do you know?"

Mary Beth grinned. "I think Pastor Mike has it bad for *you*."

"Get out!" Risa exclaimed. That was the last thing she wanted to think about at this point in time.

"It's true. I saw Pastor Mike's face last night when he carried you into the hotel."

"He carried me?" Risa was horrified.

"Well, not carried exactly. You were walking with your head on his shoulder."

"Oh, my. . ." With elbows on the table, Risa put her face in her hands.

"You said your legs felt like noodles."

"I don't remember a single thing."

"I could tell Pastor Mike was worried about you." Mary Beth paused before adding, "I was worried about you too."

Sensing the girl's sincerity, Risa's heart warmed. She glanced over at her. "You're very kind to be concerned about

me," she said, draping a sisterly arm around her shoulders.
"Thanks."

"Sure."

"However, I am embarrassed about last night. Whatever
the doctor gave me knocked me out."

"You didn't seem knocked out. You kept muttering
something like, 'I can't believe she's dead. This has to be a
nightmare.' "

Risa nodded. "And I *still* can't quite believe that Kari's. . .
gone." Tears stung her eyes, but she quickly blinked them
away.

"I want to give you something," Mary Beth said, reaching
into her backpack again. She pulled out something that
resembled a pink leather wallet. "Here."

"What is it?" Risa opened the snap in front.

"It's a Bible."

"Oh. . ." Risa wasn't sure what to say as she inspected the
silver-trimmed, tissuelike pages.

"I got it for my birthday."

"Well, I can't take this, then. You should keep it."

"No, really," Mary Beth insisted. "I want you to have it."

"Why?"

"Because. . ." The young lady seemed to grope for words.
"Because my Bible is special to me and you're special too. . .
so it just needs to go with you."

"Well, I think *you* are special."

Mary Beth dropped her gaze and shrugged.

Where's Mike when you need him? Risa wondered, looking around the food court. She didn't think she should accept
this gift, and she wasn't sure what to say to Mary Beth.

"I've got another Bible at home," the teenager said. "I like
you, and I want you to have this one."

"Maybe I'll just borrow it," Risa told her, deciding that
might be a good compromise.

"Okay." Mary Beth perked up. "If you borrow it, that

means you'd have to return it, and then I could see you again." She rummaged through her knapsack and produced a pen and paper. "I'll give you my address and phone number."

Risa laughed. She had no idea why this girl had taken such a liking to her. She hadn't done a single thing to earn Mary Beth's favor. "Are you sure you want to give me your Bible? I mean. . .what if I lose it?"

"You won't. I trust you. But I think God wants me to give it to you."

"I can buy my own Bible."

"I know," Mary Beth answered, handing her the slip of paper containing her home address. "But sometimes the Lord asks us to give away things we love to show Him that we love *Him* best."

Again, Risa didn't know how to reply. It didn't sound like God was very nice.

"My stepmom uses drugs," Mary Beth blurted, "and sometimes I believe God asks me to give up things so I can be a testimony to her and my dad. But God always repays. Like this mission trip. . .I didn't think I'd be able to go because my stepmom found the baby-sitting money I'd saved and spent it on cocaine."

Risa winced.

"I was really angry. I thought I even hated my stepmother. But then Pastor Mike asked me what I could accomplish on a mission trip if I had hatred in my heart. He said maybe my parents were my mission field, and he reminded me that God would want me to forgive my stepmom." Mary Beth smiled. "I prayed about it and realized Pastor Mike was right, so I forgave her. I told her why too. I told her God commanded me to forgive her and that He loved her. My stepmom started bawling, and I really think she was sorry she stole my money."

"So how did you end up coming to Italy?" Risa wanted to know.

"Well, see, that's the point. I gave up the idea of going,

figuring it was God's will, but someone anonymously donated the money for me to go after all. God repaid me for my sacrifice, and through it all, I was a witness for Christ."

"Quite a story," Risa remarked, although she wasn't quite sure what to make of it.

Mary Beth nodded, and in the next moment, the rest of the mission team converged on their table, grabbed surrounding chairs, and sat down.

Risa looked at her watch. "I'd better go."

"Risa!" Mike called from several feet away. He pointed to his wristwatch. "We'd better get you to your gate."

"Great minds think alike," Mary Beth quipped, wearing an impish grin. "I'll bet he's going to kiss you good-bye."

"Cut it out. . .or I'll tell Mrs. Owens what you said."

The girl's eyes grew round as bagels. "You wouldn't. . ."

"I'm kidding," Risa assured her.

Mary Beth let out a visible sigh of relief.

"What are you guys talking about?" Tracy Schmidt asked, plopping herself down in the chair beside her girlfriend.

"We're talking about lipstick and Bibles," Risa said with a wink at Mary Beth. With that she gave the girl a quick hug. "Thanks for everything."

"Sure."

Lifting her carry-on bag, Risa set it on her shoulder before making her way toward Mike.

"I can make it on my own," she told him. "You don't have to escort me to my gate."

"I know I don't *have* to," he replied with a smirk as they began to walk, "but I'd like to, if that's okay."

She grinned. "Suit yourself, Pastor."

Several paces later, he asked, "Will you let me know when Kari's funeral will be held?"

Risa nodded glumly. "But I don't think it will be much more than a memorial service. Kari's family isn't very religious."

"That's fine. I'd still like to come."

Part of her was glad to hear it, while another part of her worried that maybe Mary Beth was right and Mike did "have it bad" for her.

She glanced at him askance and had to admit to herself that over the past couple of days Mike Gerardi had proved his kind and caring ways weren't an act. His friend Wren Nickelson possessed the same characteristics, and that's what had drawn Risa to him in the first place. True gentlemen were a rare commodity in this day and age—she'd found that out the hard way.

"Just call the church and ask for me," Mike continued. "If I'm not in my office, leave a message on my voice mail."

"Will do."

They arrived at the gate, and Risa pulled her boarding pass from her satchel. "Thanks for everything, Mike. I don't know what I would have done without you these past few days." She surprised herself by realizing she meant every word.

"I'm glad I could help."

Risa turned and faced him, but one look in his eyes told her that Mary Beth's observations last night had been correct. There in the cocoa brown depths of his gaze, Risa recognized an ardent glow greater than could be explained even by friendship. Amazingly, she felt both flattered and unnerved by what she saw.

Swallowing hard, Risa said, "I think I should tell you that your whole mission team is probably spying on you."

"I figured that," Mike replied with an easy grin.

"Should we give them something to talk about, or should we just shake hands?"

Mike laughed loudly, while Risa glanced down the corridor only to find Mary Beth, Tracy, and another girl loitering near the public drinking fountain. They were as inconspicuous as a thunderstorm.

Risa decided to act quickly, mostly because she couldn't abide the awkwardness of the situation a moment longer.

Stepping toward him, she gave Mike an innocuous little hug.

"Thanks again. Have a good trip."

"Bye, Risa," she heard him say rather wistfully as she strode toward the flight attendant.

Willing herself not to look back, she handed the attendant her ticket, collected her receipt, and boarded the aircraft for home.

eight

Kari's memorial service took place the following week, on December 31. It was held, much to Risa's displeasure, in a so-called banquet room beneath the tavern where Kari's mother, Arlene, played darts every Tuesday night. Upon learning the news, Risa phoned Mike and left a message on his voice mail, telling him not to bother coming. She presumed a pastor wouldn't want to lower himself and his station by entering a rundown bar on the southeast side of Milwaukee.

But Mike surprised her by showing up, and in a suit and tie no less.

With two-year-old Jodi wiggling on her lap and Mike sitting next to her, Risa listened as, one by one, members of Kari's family stood up and shared remembrances. Some had apparently stopped in the tavern on their way to the service, because they slurred their words as they spoke fondly of the Kari they would always love and miss. Others sobbed uncontrollably.

Risa, on the other hand, saw the gathering for the farce it was. She knew these people hadn't wanted to help Kari—even when Kari had needed it most. But when Jodi's father, José, stood up and droned on in his Puerto Rican accent about how Kari would always be the love of his life and that he had wanted to marry her and make a real family for their daughter, Risa thought she would scream.

"Mike, these people are a bunch of drunken liars," she whispered when the indignation became more than she could bear.

He reached over and put a quelling hand on hers.

"José said he didn't want anything to do with Kari or Jodi. I was there when he said it!"

"Shh, Risa, not now, okay?" Mike whispered back. "We'll

66

talk about it later."

Nothing to talk about, Risa thought as anger coursed through her with each heartbeat.

Finally, it seemed everyone had taken a turn, and Risa figured the service, if it could be labeled as such, would come to an end. But it was then that Mike rose slowly from his chair.

"I'm Pastor Mike Gerardi," he began, introducing himself the same way the others had, "and I didn't know Kari very well. I met her shortly after she and Risa had been attacked in Sicily. From what I've heard, though, she accepted Jesus Christ as her Savior, which means she's living with Him in heaven today."

Risa put her nose into Jodi's soft blond hair and smiled. Leave it to a preacher to start preaching. But somehow she didn't mind the sermon tonight, realizing that Kari's relatives needed to hear it. Risa even secretly hoped Mike would elaborate about heaven, a place she guessed they knew little about. However, he astonished, perhaps even disappointed, her by making the delivery short and sweet.

"I've got some tracts here if anyone is interested in knowing how to be saved. It's the very same Bible tract Kari read." He held out several for all to see before tucking them back into the pocket of his suit jacket. Then he sat down.

"You should have let them have it," Risa said in a hushed tone. "They were listening to you. You should have told them what rotten sinners they are."

"Do you think that would have been effective with this crowd?" Mike chuckled softly. "I doubt it. Most of them are sauced. And you and I both know people can't reason in that condition."

Risa bristled at Mike's subtle reminder that she wasn't any better than Kari's family members. She noticed, too, that Mike had included himself. What did that tract say again, "For ALL have sinned. . ."? *Hard to be mad at the guy just because he's right,* she thought.

The service came to an end. Many folks left, but others stayed around to talk.

"I'll be right back," Risa told Mike.

He nodded.

Carrying Jodi across the room, she set the child down in front of Arlene. The woman looked worn beyond her years, from her thinning brown hair, gaunt face, and sunken eyes to her skinny frame.

"Where are my cigarettes, Tara?" she rasped.

"Here, Ma." Kari's rotund sister produced a pack from her pocket. Her eyes were swollen from crying. "You told me to hang onto them, remember?"

"Oh, right, where's my mind lately?" She looked at Risa. "I've been under such stress since I learned Kari died." As if to prove the statement, she swatted at an errant tear. "It's awful to lose a daughter."

"I'm sure it is," Risa said. "It's awful to lose a friend."

The woman gave Risa a hug. "Keep in touch."

She nodded. "And I'm serious about my offer to watch Jodi. Call me anytime."

"You might be sorry, because we'll probably take you up on it," Tara said, raking her plump fingers through frosted brownish-blond hair.

"That would be okay. I love Jodi."

"Thanks," Arlene said, forcing a smile. Then she glanced off, over Risa's shoulder. "Nice of that pastor to come."

Risa turned and found Mike conversing with an older gentleman.

"Who is he again?"

"A friend," she replied. "It was fortunate for Kari and me that Mike and his church group were in Palermo at the same time. I really don't know what I would have done without their support."

"Must've been really scary for you," Tara said. "I never had a friend die on me. I don't know if I'd be strong enough to cope, you know?"

By now both women drew deeply from their cigarettes. Others were smoking too, and the room began to fill with a bluish haze.

Risa saw Jodi toddling after another child, but both seemed to be supervised by the adult standing nearby. However, the sight of José talking with some friends, a shapely woman hanging on his arm, was enough to cause Risa to want to give him a piece of her mind. Talk about a hypocrite! But she had to wonder if telling the guy off would even make a difference.

"I guess I'll be leaving now," she said, swallowing her aggravation.

"Okay. We'll let you take Jodi some weekend," Arlene promised. "You're her sponsor, so you should be able to see her too."

"Thanks." With a parting smile, Risa strode over to Mike, who finished up his conversation.

"Nice to see you again, Mr. Tanner," he said before shaking the older man's hand. Turning to Risa, Mike grinned. "I always run into people I know. It's the most remarkable thing. Take that guy," he said, nodding his head at Tanner's retreating form. "He's Kari's former boss. His company did some remodeling for our church, so he recognized me tonight." Mike grinned. "Small world."

"I guess so." Risa hitched up the shoulder strap of her purse. "I'm taking off. Thanks for coming tonight."

"Hey, no sweat. I'll walk you out."

"Sure."

Risa had to smile, guessing that an invitation for pizza or cappuccino would be next on Mike's agenda. She had the guy pegged.

Grabbing her coat, she led the way up the narrow staircase and through the tavern. Risa noticed that the tavern was rapidly filling with customers. Loud country and western music blared from every corner, and tables and chairs occupied the floor space. Once outside, she breathed in the cold night air, glad to be out of the stuffy barroom.

"My car's parked across the street," she told Mike, who now walked beside her.

When they reached her midsized silver car, Risa paused to fish her keys from her purse.

"Have you seen your family since you've been back?" Mike wanted to know.

"Yep. The big news is still my cousin's upcoming wedding. She and I shopped last night and looked at bridesmaids' dresses." Risa stopped short of telling him that she'd felt totally depressed on the way home. She wished she'd been shopping for her own big day. Then Kari's funeral service—or whatever it was—didn't help her dampened spirits in the least.

"I take it your relatives know what happened in Sicily."

"Yes. I told my grandmother the whole story, and she must have spread the news. No one has asked about my trip. I don't know if that makes things easier or harder for me."

"Do you feel like you need to discuss the situation with someone? I mean, it was a rather traumatic experience for you."

"No, I'm okay."

"Well, if you change your mind, we've got trained counselors on staff if you need to talk," he offered. "Their sessions are free."

Risa gave him a polite smile, thinking he looked quite stylish in his heavy black wool coat. "Thanks, but I think I'm all right. However," she added seriously, "I'll keep it in mind. I start a new job on Tuesday, so my stress level is, like, at its peak."

"I imagine so." With furrowed brows, he leaned up against her car, his arms folded in front of him, his hands clad in leather gloves. "I didn't know you had a new job."

"Yep. It's at South Bend Mutual Life downtown. I'm the

new manager of its customer service center."

"Congratulations."

"Thanks. . .I think."

Mike chuckled. "When did this happen?"

"Almost six weeks ago. Right after Wren's book signing in Appleton. . .you know, the one you told me about?" Risa smiled at the startled expression on Mike's face. "Didn't you know I went to see Wren at his signing?"

"No, I didn't." Now Mike looked concerned.

"I went to say. . .good-bye. And to get his autograph, of course."

"Of course."

"You don't believe me, do you? Well, it's the truth. I'm happy for Wren. He made his decision, and it's final. But I wanted a chance at a new life too, and making the effort to say *arrivederci* and then quitting at the post office was all part of taking that first step and moving on. But if what happened in Italy is any indication of what the rest of my life is going to be like," she said, tears pooling in her eyes, "I might as well slit my wrists now."

"Don't talk like that, Risa."

She whirled around and tried to stick her car key into the lock, but through bleary eyes she failed.

Mike caught her wrist. "Hey, I believe you. If you went to say good-bye to Wren, that's your business. What's more, I'm downright impressed. Most people don't have the courage to attempt the new starts you've made."

Risa shrugged.

"Look, what do you say we go get a pizza, huh?"

She laughed, sniffing back her tears. "You're very predictable, know that?"

"What?" Mike dropped his hand, looking puzzled.

"But that's okay," she said, pulling a tissue from the pocket of her winter coat. She dried her eyes. "Predictable has its merits."

"Risa, all I know is I'm hungry, and my cousin has this great Italian restaurant on North Avenue."

"It's New Year's Eve. Won't it be crowded? Don't we need reservations?"

"Naw, my cousin John will find a table for us." He tipped his head curiously. "Have other plans tonight?"

"No. I was just planning to stay home and feel sorry for myself," she quipped, although it wasn't too far from the truth. She certainly wasn't in a party mood.

"Well, how 'bout dinner with a friend who cares about you? Isn't that better than sitting home alone?"

His words plucked a tender cord on her heartstrings. "You're a sweet guy, Mike."

He shrugged, looking somewhat embarrassed.

"Okay, dinner it is. Get in your car and let's go. I'll follow you."

Grinning like a boy on his birthday, he backed away a few steps, then turned and jogged across the street to his vehicle.

Shaking her head after him, Risa unlocked her car and climbed in.

nine

Mike tiptoed through his apartment, careful not to disturb his cousin Claudio, who was visiting from Italy. Reaching his bedroom, he glanced at the neon numbers on his clock radio: 3:00.

Mike winced. He had to be at church for their annual New Year's Day rally with the elementary-age kids in four hours.

He shucked off his clothes, tossing his tie, shirt, and trousers onto the wooden valet near his bed. Then he pulled on a pair of gym shorts and an old T-shirt. Quietly walking to the bathroom, he brushed his teeth, gargled, and returned to his room. Turning off the light and crawling under the bedcovers, he then stared at the dark ceiling. It didn't take much to discern that he was in dangerous waters and heading for the falls.

Risa. If he hadn't been in love with her before, he certainly was now.

I know, Lord—she's not a Christian. I've got no business pursuing her.

Suddenly he recalled a class he'd taken during seminary. One of the topics had been choosing a godly "helpmeet," and the instructor, a crusty old Southerner, had listed several qualifications that a man in the ministry should look for.

Risa didn't meet a single one. She hadn't gone to Bible college, hadn't been reared in a Christian home, and she wasn't called to full-time service. First and foremost. . .she wasn't saved!

Mike sighed. But on the other hand, his cousin seemed to like her. John and his wife were relatively new believers, and they had sat down with Mike and Risa after the restaurant closed at twelve-thirty. The four of them ate, talked, and laughed for the next two hours. What's more, Mike got a glimpse of the real Risa, her candid side—the part of her personality that she'd displayed on the first night he'd met her. Outspoken, witty, courageous, yet sensitive, she'd won him over for the second time.

Mike rolled onto his left side. Attraction and admiration were well and good. He and Risa had had a good time tonight. But the fact remained, she wasn't a believer. Furthermore, he shouldn't have kissed her in the parking lot.

I know, I know, Lord, but I couldn't help it.

There she'd stood under the street lamp, all pink-lipped and gazing up at him with those bright hazel eyes. Dainty snowflakes were falling from the sky, and they stuck on her nose and lashes. It had been a scene straight out of his favorite daydreams.

"Happy New Year, Mike," she said in a come-hither tone that tugged at his being.

"Happy New Year. . . ."

And the next thing he knew, he'd pulled her into a snug embrace, his lips on hers. He tasted the peppermint from the spumoni she'd eaten; he smelled the delicate scent of her perfume. In a word, he was lost. Time stood still, and in those brief moments, nothing mattered. He was like a drowning man, going down for the last time, helpless to save himself.

When the kiss ended, Risa had wrapped her arms around his neck. "You know, Mike," she'd murmured, "I needed that kiss. I've been feeling so depressed lately."

He'd stood there, his hands around her waist, and gazed down at her lovely face. She had appeared vulnerable, and he'd longed to kiss her again. But in the next moment, she let go of him and stepped back.

"To tell you the truth, I didn't think a pastor could kiss like that."

Mike had seen the teasing, almost flirtatious gleam in her eyes. It had been a stroke for his ego, and he grinned at the memory. However, he quickly wiped the grin off his face. This was no laughing matter. And he realized the precariousness of his situation. A man could fall so fast, so fast.

I'm sorry, Father, he prayed. *I wasn't exactly the greatest example for Risa tonight, was I?*

In addition to protecting his testimony, Mike wanted to protect Risa too. From what she'd alluded to tonight, as they'd discussed various personal topics, she'd been hurt too many times in the past. He wasn't about to break her heart again. He just couldn't let that happen.

Okay, Lord, I know I got myself into this mess. I'm sorry about it. Forgive me, Mike prayed earnestly. *And now I ask that You give me wisdom to somehow work this situation out to Your honor and glory. In Jesus' name. . .Amen.*

❧

The month of January blew into Wisconsin on gusts of frosty weather and more snow. Risa found herself grateful to be working in a warm office, as opposed to her old job of managing a cold postal station, occasionally delivering mail in inclement weather. Nevertheless, after her fourth day at the insurance company, she came home to her apartment and collapsed on the sofa. She'd put in another twelve-hour day. She hoped South Bend Mutual wasn't going to expect this from her all the time; she had to believe things would calm down once she understood her responsibilities. But one thing seemed certain: Her job at the post office was a lot easier— even in freezing winter weather. Of course, she'd been there for over ten years. However, she hadn't been required to wear skirts, blouses, business suits, and heels.

Risa kicked off her shoes and rubbed her aching feet. Then picking up the mail in her lap, she looked over each envelope. Bills, bills, and more bills. Nothing interesting.

The phone rang, and she decided she felt too tired to get up and answer it. Instead, she let her machine take the call. Unless it was Mike, she stipulated; in that case, she might spring for the phone.

"Hi, this is Arlene," came the familiar raspy voice.

Mild disappointment filled Risa. She hadn't heard from Mike in more than a week now. Oddly, a portion of her heart didn't want him to call, either—not that Mike wasn't a kind, considerate guy. But he was a pastor, and that still troubled Risa. She knew nothing about living a Christian lifestyle. On the other hand, part of Risa enjoyed Mike's attention and companionship.

"I want to know if you can watch Jodi this weekend. I'm going snowmobiling up north, and I can't get a hold of José."

"Surprise, surprise," Risa muttered.

"I'll be gone a week," the woman said, "and I can't take her with me up to the cabin. It's not exactly baby-proof, you know? Since it's my boyfriend's place, I can't very well ask him to rearrange his house for a toddler."

Risa sighed, feeling none too sympathetic.

"I don't know what your work schedule is, but maybe you could take a week's vacation and watch Jodi."

"Yeah, right!" she grumbled.

"Call me back." Arlene rattled off her number and then hung up the phone. The machine clicked off.

Risa moaned. The last thing she felt like doing was watching a two year old this weekend. Sleeping for forty-eight hours sounded much more appealing. And what about next week? She had to work. Long hours too.

But she had made a promise, and if Kari could look down from heaven, she'd be justifiably disappointed if Risa didn't stick to her word.

So what do I do? she wondered.

Her cousin's wife, Therese, came to mind. She lived in Brookfield, a good forty-five-minute drive away, but she was home all day with her kids. Maybe Therese would watch Jodi next week while Risa worked. Of course, she would probably have to pay her.

Risa considered the idea for several long minutes. She didn't have much spare cash. But if she promised to cook a late dinner for her cousin's family every night, maybe that would suffice as payment. Matthew, her cousin, always touted Risa's cooking as "to die for."

It was worth a shot.

Rousing herself from the couch, Risa made the call. After explaining the situation, Therese agreed to care for Jodi. The next phone call went to Arlene, who sounded overjoyed by the news.

They made all the necessary arrangements.

Hanging up the telephone, Risa looked at the small clock on her living-room desk. It was nearly ten. She stood, and, feeling too tired to eat dinner, she walked into her room and prepared for bed. Again she wondered why Mike hadn't contacted her. The way he'd behaved last week, Risa thought she'd hear from him every day.

Climbing into bed, she switched on the television, intending to watch the late news. Like a flash, she knew why she hadn't heard from Mike.

He can't date anyone who's not a Christian.

Wren had informed her of that "rule" more than once, even though Risa hadn't understood it. Except. . .wasn't she a Christian now that she'd given her soul to God? She knew she wasn't perfect—she was a sinner in God's eyes. She understood Jesus was the only one who could save her from that sin and that He had done so by dying on the cross. Wasn't this what constituted being "born again," the term Mike had used for being a Christian?

Remembering the pink wallet-sized Bible that Mary Beth had given her, Risa crawled from beneath her quilt and went in search of it. She found the Book on the kitchen counter beside five rolls of film that she still couldn't bring herself to develop. She wasn't ready to see Kari's face, hamming it up during their ill-fated vacation.

Ignoring the film, Risa picked up the Bible and took it back to bed with her.

So, where does a person start reading? she wondered, flipping through the delicate, tissuelike pages. She wasn't familiar with the Bible, although if she recalled correctly, the priests at church had read from the Gospels during mass. But to her shame, Risa had to admit that she'd never paid much attention. Furthermore, her family wasn't very religious—not even Nana, who attended church perhaps once or twice a year.

At last she decided to treat the Book like any other, and she started at the beginning. She skimmed through the preface and the next few pages that listed each book of the Bible. Then she came to Genesis and read, "In the beginning, God created the heavens and earth. Now the earth was formless and empty, darkness was over the surface of the deep, and the Spirit of God was hovering over the waters. And God said, 'Let there be light,' and there was light. . . ."

❧

Sitting behind his desk, Mike drummed out a nervous beat with the end of his pen as he stared at the telephone. Nearly a week and a half had gone by and he hadn't called Risa— mainly because he didn't think he had a right to. But after much prayer, he came up with the perfect idea for an appropriate "date." He would invite Risa to church tomorrow and lunch at his sister's house afterward. Of course, he'd thrown out this same invitation once before, more than a year ago, and Risa had refused it. Would she do so again?

Mike set down his pen and decided to get it over with. The worst Risa could say was "no"—and he kind of figured that's the reply he'd get.

Flipping open his address book, he found Risa's name and dialed her number. She picked up in two rings.

"Risa! Hi, it's Mike. How ya doin'?"

"Oh, hi." There was a smile in her voice and perhaps an element of surprise. "I'm okay. How 'bout you?"

"Been busy." He reclined in his desk chair. "We had an all-night youth rally last night. Held it in the gym and invited a bunch of kids from the local high school. Altogether, including our youth group, there were about fifty teenagers. We played volleyball, basketball, ate pizza, and showed a movie that had a clear gospel presentation. . . ." Mike yawned. "Then we played more basketball, volleyball, and ate more pizza. I didn't get much sleep."

"Fifty kids, huh? And I'm going bananas with just one." She laughed. "Hang on a sec."

Risa dropped the receiver and Mike could hear her talking to someone—a child, obviously. "Hi, I'm back. I'm watching Jodi, and she was about to scale my lower kitchen cabinets. She already emptied them. But I've got her looking at a book now." She sighed, sounding winded. "Kids are a lot of work!"

"Yeah, I hear my sister say that all the time." Mike chuckled. "Speaking of work, how's the new job going?"

"Good, as far as I can tell, having only completed my first week."

"Think you'll like it?"

"Time will tell, I guess. . . . Jodi, no, no, don't rip the book." Risa paused. "Hang on, Mike."

He waited once again until she had successfully distracted the little girl.

"I've got her coloring now," Risa said. "That'll hold her attention for the next two minutes. We'd better talk fast."

"Okay." Mike felt anxious flutters suddenly fill his gut. "I called to, um, ask if you'd come to church tomorrow and then have lunch with me at my sister Patti's place."

"Well, I've got Jodi all weekend."

"Bring her along. There are nurseries at church, and my sister has enough kids to entertain Jodi tomorrow afternoon."

"Um. . ."

While she took a moment to think about it, Mike held his breath and prayed.

"Okay, sure."

"Sure?" Mike didn't think he'd heard correctly. "You'll come?"

"Yeah, I'll come." Risa laughed softly. "Did you think I'd say no?"

"I was praying you wouldn't."

"Hmm. . ." She paused. "I want to ask you something."

Mike grinned and felt himself relax. "Okay, shoot."

"Where can I buy a Bible? Will pretty much any bookstore carry them?"

She wants to buy a Bible?

Mike blinked and then shook his head in disbelief. "Well, um, yeah, you can find Bibles in just about any bookstore," he replied, trying to overcome his shock. "But there's more of a selection at a Christian store." He gave her the names of the shops he knew of in the area.

"Great. I've got some running around to do this morning, so I can swing by any one of those stores." Risa paused. "Mike, you wouldn't believe what Jodi has been sleeping in—it's a dirty, beat-up wooden playpen that I wouldn't stick my dog in, let alone a child. So I'm buying one of those portable cribs for when she stays with me. And Arlene was out of diapers, so I have to stock up on them.

"We're okay on clothes, though. Arlene went over to Kari's place and collected most of Jodi's things, but no one has even begun to clean out Kari's apartment. Overall, Mike, I'm disgusted with her family and the way they're handling this situation." She halted momentarily. "I'm rambling, and I apologize," she said. "It's just that I've been upset since picking up Jodi last night."

"Hey, ramble all you want. That's what friends are for, right?" Mike wished he could keep her talking to him all day.

She gave a little laugh. "Right. Thanks. But I guess I'll have to vent another time. Jodi just decided to use her crayons on my glass-topped end table."

"Uh-oh." Mike grinned, imagining the scenario.

"I'll see you tomorrow."

"The worship service begins at ten-fifteen," he added quickly. "Do you remember how to get to the church?"

"Yep."

"All right, then. Bye for now."

Mike hung up the phone. "Thank You, God!" he shouted with hands raised high in the air. "What a blessing!"

As he mulled over his conversation with Risa, he couldn't get over how different she sounded this morning. Quite a change from the woman he'd run into in Palermo. Weeks ago, she had dodged any discussion of religion. Now she wanted to buy a Bible.

Mike's spirit soared. This could only mean one thing, he decided. God was at work in that woman's heart!

ten

Despite her promise to attend what Mike called "worship service," Risa felt overwhelmed and even anxious when she reached Bay Community Church Sunday morning. She considered changing her mind, but she knew she'd never hear the end of it. Besides, if Mike's sister had gone out of her way to prepare lunch today, Risa would feel downright rude for standing her up.

With renewed determination, she unfastened Jodi from the car seat and grabbed the diaper bag. Hanging onto Jodi's hand, Risa opened the trunk and checked on the chocolate cake she'd baked last night. Since she disliked showing up at someone's house empty-handed, even if she had been invited, Risa had whipped up her favorite chocolate cake recipe. She hoped her hostess would appreciate it.

Locking the car, Risa led the toddler to the side door of the church. Inside she took off Jodi's snowsuit, then hung up her own coat. She felt foolish asking directions to the nursery; however, everyone seemed more than willing to help.

"Bye, Sweetie," Risa said, giving Jodi a kiss and a hug. "You be a good girl."

"Where you going?" the little girl asked, looking up at her with huge brown eyes.

"To church. But I'll be back in a little while, okay?"

Jodi frowned, looking uncertain, and Risa's heart ached. No doubt Kari had said the same thing before leaving for Italy. Kari never thought she wouldn't return to see her daughter again.

Then last night, Risa had thought her heart would shatter when Jodi asked, "Where my mommy go?" Obviously the toddler missed her mother and couldn't conceptualize never seeing her again.

"Your mommy's with Jesus," Risa had replied, not knowing how else to explain Kari's absence. "She's in a wonderful place called heaven."

The answer seemed the simplest of replies, and one, perhaps, that a child would accept—at least Risa had hoped.

And it worked.

"I go heaven too," Jodi said with a determined look on her small face.

With that, the child let the subject drop, much to Risa's relief.

Gazing down at the little girl now clinging to Risa's tailored green linen skirt, Risa wondered if she should just take Jodi to church with her.

"She'll be fine," the stout nursery worker assured Risa. "We're going to paint this morning and sing songs." The older woman with graying blond hair hunkered in front of Jodi while listing the planned activities. "And we're going to have a snack and hear a story. Wouldn't you like to stay?"

Jodi looked up at Risa.

"Go ahead, Sweetie," she said. "It'll be fun, and then I'll come and pick you up in an hour or so."

The toddler hesitated, and the nursery worker quickly took advantage of the moment. "C'mon, Jodi. Look at these toys."

Leading the little girl to the bright plastic bin of playthings, the woman shooed Risa away with a wave and a kind smile.

She backed away from the nursery feeling somewhat guilty, but she decided Jodi was in capable hands. Turning, she made her way to the sanctuary and found a seat.

While she got comfortable, Risa allowed her gaze to wander about her surroundings until she spotted Leslie Owens. The tall, slim blond stood near the front by the piano, talking with another woman. Risa noticed that Leslie's hair was in its prudent little coil, and she couldn't help but think the woman would be ever so much more attractive if she'd unloose that knot. Glancing around once more, Risa didn't see anyone else she recognized.

She had attended one other service here at Bay Community Church, but didn't have fond memories of the event. This had been Wren's church, and although she'd never accepted his invitation to come here, she did accept Mike's—when Wren was out of town one weekend. She'd been curious, wondering what their religion was all about and why it differed from everything she'd been taught growing up. But Risa had returned home that day just as puzzled as ever.

Oddly, a lot of things were beginning to make sense now.

Catching sight of Mike and watching him pause to speak with Leslie, Risa recalled Mary Beth saying that the woman "had it bad" for him. So how come he didn't ask Leslie out? Or maybe he did, Risa mused, and maybe he found he just wasn't interested in her.

Maybe he's interested in me.

No, he just wants me to be a born-again Christian.

As if to point out the contrary, the kiss they had shared almost two weeks ago suddenly popped into her mind. She grinned to herself, deciding that she meant more to Mike than another notch in his Bible cover. Even so, Risa didn't quite know how to handle it. . .or him.

"Hi, Miss Vitalis!"

Risa shook herself from her reverie and saw Mary Beth standing in the aisle, peering down at her with a wide smile.

"Well, hi yourself."

"Are you feeling better? You look better."

"Yes, I am. Thanks."

Mary Beth nodded to the place beside Risa. "Can I sit with you?"

"Sure."

The teenager scooted into the pew and sat down. At that

moment, Risa remembered Mary Beth's Bible and her promise to return it.

Opening her purse, Risa pulled out the slim Book. "I hoped I'd see you today. Here." At the girl's hesitant expression, Risa added, "I bought my own Bible. See?"

Risa lifted the burgundy leather-bound Word of God. "It's called the Rainbow Bible, and it has three translations in it, each in different colors. There's also a day-to-day reading schedule with short applications after each one."

"That's awesome!" Mary Beth declared.

"When I heard it was called the Rainbow Bible, I knew I had to buy it."

"How come?"

"Oh. . ." Risa hedged, uncertain if she could share what had become a terribly personal experience. "It's just something that happened in Sicily."

"When your friend died?"

Risa nodded, recalling the rainbow stretched across the sky, seemingly just for her. "It happened the very morning she died."

"I see. . . ." Mary Beth looked down forlornly at her pink, leather-bound Bible and then tucked it into the nylon bag she carried along with her purse. "Your friend is in a better place, Miss Vitalis," she said at last, "but that doesn't make things any easier on you, does it?"

Risa didn't know how to reply. "In a way, I guess it is easier. Although I don't imagine death is ever an easy thing to take. I'm fortunate in that I haven't experienced a lot of death in my family. No one close to me, besides my friend Kari, has died."

"Well, good. Then there's still time to witness to them."

Bringing her chin back, Risa regarded the girl with surprise. Her expression implied that what had come out of her mouth was the most natural thing ever. To Risa, on the other hand, the thought of "witnessing" to her family members seemed a foreign and forbidding task. What would she say? Would they listen?

"Hi, can I sit with you too?"

Swinging her gaze to the left, Risa saw a young lady standing in the aisle next to her pew. Her fawn brown hair hung in waves to her shoulders, and her amber eyes sparkled with enthusiasm.

"I'm Tracy," she said. "Do you remember me from the mission trip? I'm Mary Beth's friend."

"Oh, right." In truth, Risa couldn't place the girl because she'd been in such a harried state after Kari died. But she didn't want to hurt Tracy's feelings. "Sure, you're welcome to sit with us."

"Great."

Smiling, Tracy climbed over Risa, taking a seat on the other side of Mary Beth. Then she leaned over and whispered something that caused both girls to giggle.

"What's so funny?" Risa asked, inclining her head toward them.

Tracy did her best to wipe the grin off her face. "Pastor Mike said to leave some room for him."

Risa sat up straight and shook her head at the girls. "Whatever."

They laughed again, and it was hard for Risa to remember what being fifteen had been like, since it meant turning the clock back twenty years. But even if that were possible, she had a difficult time trying to imagine herself being as naive as these two sitting beside her. Risa had gone out with her first boyfriend in seventh grade and had had a steady stream of suitors ever since. Unfortunately, none turned out to be keepers.

A couple of quick glances at Mary Beth and Tracy, now obviously whispering about the boy sitting two rows in front of them, and Risa felt certain she'd never been as young as the two of them. Not at fifteen. Not ever. She'd been thrust into adulthood before her teenage years ever began. She used to think of herself as being sophisticated, worldly. But now she wondered if she hadn't been robbed of a large portion of her childhood.

Leslie Owens began to play the piano and the pews filled with more people. Minutes later, the music stopped and a man walked to the front podium.

"Good morning, everyone."

"Good morning," came the unanimous reply.

"Sounds like you're all still sleeping," he teased. "Let's try it once more. *Good morning*, everyone."

He was rewarded with a much more enthusiastic response.

Risa had to smile, and she thought she recognized the man in the pulpit as the head pastor of this church. Clad in a charcoal gray, pinstriped suit, he looked as dapper as any of the businessmen at South Bend Mutual.

"For those who are visiting, I'm Pastor Kevin Batzler."

Risa silently congratulated herself for correctly guessing the man's identity.

The pastor continued with his welcoming address before introducing Mike, who he said wanted to make some announcements.

Mike went forward, stood at the podium, and began to speak. As he did so, his gaze roamed over the congregation until it fell on Risa. In that fraction of a moment, his eyes seemed to caress her so tenderly, so intensely, that she had to look away. Peering down at her hands, folded on top of her Bible, Risa would have convinced herself that she'd imagined the whole thing. After all, Mike never missed a syllable. Except Mary Beth elbowed her.

"He likes you," she whispered, grinning like a Cheshire cat.

Embarrassed, Risa elbowed her right back. "Hush."

Mary Beth looked contrite, so Risa gave her a smile and an affectionate wink.

Unfortunately, she didn't hear a word of the announcements. Mike left the podium and another man took the stand.

"That's our music director," Mary Beth whispered. "Singing to the Lord is the way we worship Him before we hear the preaching."

"I see," Risa said politely. She thought it was nice of the girl to point out the order of the service.

"Turn to page 339 in your hymnals, please," the music director said.

Risa found the hymn and then stood with the rest of the congregation. While Leslie accompanied them on the piano, Risa tried to sing along. She'd never in her life heard this song before: "O Love That Wilt Not Let Me Go." But she caught on to the melody rather quickly and felt surprised when tears pricked her eyes while she sang the third verse.

> O Joy that seekest me thru pain,
> I cannot close my heart to Thee,
> I trace the rainbow thru the rain,
> And feel the promise is not vain.
> That mourn shall tearless be.

Suddenly something else made sense—something Leslie had said about God's promises being like a rainbow in the rain.

Risa glanced at the hymn once again and read the words, "The promise is not vain. . . ."

"So that's what it meant."

"What?" Mary Beth leaned closer. "What did you say?"

Risa shook her head. "Nothing," she fibbed.

However, it was a far cry from "nothing." Risa had just figured out God's message to her that day in Sicily. With the rainbow. He was showing her how real He was and that He kept His promises.

And in that moment, Risa never felt surer of God's special love for her. He really cared. . .and in such a personal way.

"Personal Savior." Hadn't she heard that phrase before? She just hadn't known what it meant. But she understood now. That's what this born-again business was all about. . .a personal relationship with God. . .with Jesus. Of course, Wren had told her that a hundred times; she just didn't get it then.

But she got it now.

"I've got it," she muttered. She looked at Mary Beth and smiled. "I've got it!"

eleven

"What have you got?" Mike asked, stepping into the pew and standing beside Risa. He had overheard her exclamation and couldn't help but be curious.

The congregation sat down.

"I'll tell you later," Risa whispered in reply.

Mike nodded just as Kevin walked to the pulpit.

"Take your Bibles and turn to the first epistle of John," he said.

Finding his place, Mike watched as Risa looked in her Bible's table of contents before locating the book of Scripture. He sat amazed; this was a different Risa than he'd ever seen before, one who followed along with the message, one who'd purchased her own Bible.

Mike rejoiced in the remarkable change, knowing only God could accomplish such a feat. The last time Risa attended this church, she'd said, "This religion stuff isn't for me." Next she'd told Mike to "have a nice life" before exiting the building. Of course, he'd been hurt, but that didn't keep him from calling Risa every so often in an effort to keep in touch. And then, in Palermo, Risa had stormed from the coffeehouse during Mike's testimony.

But she wasn't running away now. She was listening.

I love her, Lord. I've got no reasonable basis for loving her, but I can't help it.

Risa touched his arm, drawing him from his musings.

"I don't understand, Mike," she whispered. "How do we stay away from the world when we're part of the world?"

He gave her a patient smile. "It's kind of involved," he told her in hushed tones. "I'll explain after church."

90

"Okay."

His smile grew, and Mike decided he'd better pay attention to Kevin's message, since he had a hunch Risa would have more questions.

❧

Mike's sister, Patti Kreske, and her husband, David, lived in Bayside, about five minutes from the church. Risa followed the Kreskes' maroon minivan to their home, since Mike had been detained by Leslie Owens—who said she *had* to speak with him immediately. In a way, Leslie reminded Risa of herself, although not in the physical sense. In that regard, they were opposites. Where Leslie had flawless, china-doll skin, Risa had freckles—everywhere. Leslie's blond hair was naturally straight, whereas Risa's red hair was, for the most part, unruly. But there were similar personality traits that Risa had picked up on. For instance, Leslie didn't mince words; she spoke her mind. Risa had seen that at the hotel in Sicily. And when the woman wanted something, she went after it. . .and if Risa didn't think so before, she knew now that Leslie was after Mike.

Oddly, that fact didn't bother Risa a bit, and she wondered if she'd grown tired of competing for a man's love. It was her life's story, and it always happened that someone else triumphed over her. Like Nancie Nickelson. . .and a host of others who'd come before her. They got the guy and Risa walked away, tending her broken heart. Then again, maybe there wasn't anything left of her heart to break.

From the backseat, Jodi babbled away sweetly, and Risa smiled. The little girl had enjoyed "school" this morning, and she'd been in a happy mood ever since. That alone made Risa want to go back to Bay Community Church next Sunday. Perhaps she could arrange to keep Jodi every weekend. Knowing Kari's mother, that wouldn't be a problem.

Stopping at a red light, Risa continued her musing. The pastor's message today had been quite uplifting. Motivational, in fact. She wondered if Pastor Batzler scheduled speaking engagements. Risa thought her department at work could use some encouragement.

The light turned green, and Risa pressed her foot against the accelerator. Within a few minutes, she saw the minivan signal and make a right turn. Risa followed. A block later, it was a left turn into the Kreskes' driveway.

"Mike had better not miss lunch," Patti said, unbuckling her younger children from their car seats. "I'll never speak to him again if he doesn't show up. I put a roast in the oven before I left."

Risa smiled politely and then unloosed Jodi, who ran through the snow after one of Patti's kids.

"Relax, Honey," David said. "He'll show up. Might be late, but he'll show. He always does."

"Well, there's always a first time, you know?"

With a laugh, the tall, dark-headed man sauntered to the front door and unlocked it. The children filed in behind him.

Pulling her chocolate cake out of the cardboard nest she'd created in the trunk, Risa walked to the house with Patti. She'd already decided that both the Kreskes resembled typical Italians. Dark hair, dark eyes, olive skin—but it was poor Patti who'd inherited that classic Roman nose. And with a last name like Kreske, Risa had to assume David had gotten his Mediterranean features from his mother's side of the family.

"You didn't need to bring anything," Patti said, eyeing the container Risa carried.

"I love to cook and bake, so you'll have to forgive me for using your invitation today as an excuse to whip up a chocolate cake. It's my grandmother's favorite."

"Can't wait to try a piece."

After hanging up their coats, Risa followed Patti through the house and into the kitchen. She set down the round, covered cake tin on the counter.

"Make yourself at home," Patti said. "The kids are already

in the backyard. It's fenced in, so you don't have to worry about your little girl." Opening the patio doors, Patti called to her oldest child, "Hey, Delaney, keep your eye on Jodi, okay?"

Patti turned to Risa. "My oldest daughter, Delaney, is such a little mother. She's only ten, but she loves to baby-sit. . .as long as the kids aren't her siblings. But I don't blame her. I hated taking care of my brothers and sisters. They never listened to me. Especially Mike. What a brat he was!"

Risa grinned, thinking of "Madman Mike" as a little boy, wreaking havoc among his siblings.

"Frankly, I can't wait till Mike gets married and has kids, because I believe the Bible, and God says a man reaps what he sows." Patti laughed. "Mike's in for trouble with a capital T, and as his oldest sister, I'm going to sit back and laugh my head off."

"Does Mike want to get married and have kids?" Risa asked, taking a seat at Patti's kitchen table.

"Yeah, I think he does. It's hard on a guy in the ministry when he's not married."

"How come?"

"Well, for one thing, he's always getting set up on blind dates or, rather, surprise dates. Once a sweet older couple at church invited him over for lunch and, what a coincidence!—they just happened to have their single niece staying with them that weekend."

Risa chuckled, picturing the scene.

"Mike's found himself in some pretty tight jams, so it's a good thing he's a fast talker."

"And a convincing one at that," Risa added, recalling all the times Mike had cajoled her into going out for pizza or coffee. . .or to church. "So, I hear Leslie Owens is vying for the wife position Mike's got open."

Patti lifted an inquiring brow. "How'd you find that out?"

Risa grinned. "I'd better not reveal my source."

"You're a smart woman. Where would we be without our

sources, eh?" Smiling, Patti opened the refrigerator and pulled out a bag of salad mix. "Well, I can tell you what *my* source said about the situation: He's not interested! Leslie's wasting her time."

Risa grew suddenly solemn. Looking down at the flowered place mat in front of her, she felt a little sorry for Leslie. She knew how it felt to be "wasting time" loving a man who would never love her in return.

"Hey, cheer up over there," Patti said, as if sensing Risa's melancholy. "I don't think you're in the same category as Leslie, okay?"

"Get that from your *source*, did you?" Risa quipped.

"Yeah, I did. So there."

Risa smiled, then laughed out loud. And in that instant, she decided she liked Patti Kreske.

"So, um, what do you think of my brother?"

With elbows on the table, Risa set her chin in her palms. "I think you just asked the million-dollar question."

"Meaning you're not sure about him?"

Risa shrugged.

"You dating somebody else?"

"No."

"Are you in love with somebody else?"

"No." Risa didn't even hesitate to answer that question. And it surprised her to discover that she really meant it, which was a good thing in her mind. It signified that she no longer harbored false hopes about Wren.

"Okay, you're two for two, Risa."

She laughed.

"Do you. . .like my brother?"

"I like him fine, it's just that I don't think I'm qualified to be a pastor's wife."

"Hey, I can understand that. But once I overheard Julie Batzler talking to a woman who'd inquired over *her* credentials, so to speak. She said all a pastor's wife has to do is be in love with the pastor. The rest falls into place." Breaking open the bag of lettuce, Patti poured it into a wooden salad bowl. "To me, I think marrying a pastor would be like being a doctor's wife, or a lawyer's wife. . .or the wife of a businessman. I mean, there are adjustments to be made in any given situation."

Risa shrugged. "Yeah, maybe."

"So. . .think you're cut out to be a doctor's wife?"

Dropping her head back, Risa laughed. "I'm pleading the Fifth on that one."

"Coward."

"Well, I see you two are getting along just fine," David said, entering the kitchen. He'd changed his clothes; jeans and a long-sleeved blue polo shirt now replaced his suit and tie. "Two Italian women in the same kitchen. . .ah!"

He feigned a horrified expression.

"But if you'll notice, only one of us is cooking," Patti replied on a tart note.

"It's not that I didn't offer to help," Risa couldn't help throwing in.

David chuckled.

"Hey, is the food done? I'm starved." Mike's voice boomed from the direction of the front door.

Patti narrowed her gaze at Risa. "Typical male. No 'Hello,' just 'Feed me.' "

Risa smirked, thinking that pretty much summed it up.

At that moment, Mike walked into the kitchen. He smiled a greeting at Risa, kissed Patti, and then turned and shook hands with his brother-in-law.

"Hope I didn't miss anything," he said with a charming grin.

"No. I was just grilling Risa," Patti stated nonchalantly.

Mike's wide-eyed and worried stare met Risa's gaze.

She gave him an assured wink. Everything was fine.

One of the Kreske boys entered through the patio doors, depositing clumps of snow on the kitchen floor. His cheeks were as red as cherries. "Mom, are we going to eat soon? I'm hungry."

"What'd I tell you, Risa? That's male mentality for you. I guess I'd better serve our meal before I have a riot on my hands."

While Patti busied herself with setting the dining-room table and David rounded up the kids, Risa watched Mike lift the cake's lid and snitch a fingerful of chocolate frosting.

"I saw that," she said.

"Well, just don't tell my sister you saw it," he replied quietly.

She thought it over. "Hmm. . .what sort of bribe could I come up with?"

Mike grinned, but it didn't quite alight in his eyes.

"I was just kidding."

He shook his head. "It's not you or what you said. The word 'bribe' just made me think about my conversation with. . .oh, forget it."

Risa narrowed her gaze, knowing he'd just come from talking with Leslie. "Don't tell me Leslie Owens is trying to—"

"No, no. . .and I guess bribe wasn't the right word." He arched a brow, seeming aggravated, and Risa didn't think she'd ever seen Mike look anything but happy and easygoing. "Threat seems to fit."

"She threatened you? With what?"

"You."

"Me?" Risa couldn't believe it. She frowned. "How?"

Mike glanced in the direction of the dining room. "Let's discuss it after lunch, okay?"

"Sure." Her frown deepened as incredulity filled her being. What was that woman thinking?

Feeling suddenly warm and constrained, Risa stood and slipped off the hunter green linen jacket she wore. This morning, she'd chosen to wear one of the business suits she purchased before starting her new job. She didn't have much else in the way of church clothes.

She hung the jacket over the kitchen chair and looked up in time to catch Mike's appreciative gaze. Her cheeks warmed with embarrassment, and she looked back down at her jacket.

I shouldn't be so embarrassed, she thought, feeling oddly flustered.

"Green is a nice color on you," he remarked. "Complements your hazel eyes."

He knows the color of my eyes? Risa felt momentarily stunned. One guy she'd dated for over two years hadn't even known that. He'd made the mistake of saying her eyes were brown. After that, their relationship fizzled out because, to Risa's way of thinking, he obviously hadn't been interested in her as a person.

But Mike had noticed her eye color—and they weren't even officially dating.

"Thanks," Risa said, lifting her gaze. "You know what, Pastor Gerardi? You surprise me at every turn."

Mike stepped forward and took hold of the back of an adjacent chair. "Is that good?"

Risa mulled it over. "I haven't decided yet."

He chuckled and appeared somewhat chagrined. "What did you think of the service this morning?"

"In a word, I'd have to call it encouraging."

Mike smiled. "Glad you thought so."

The kids came bursting into the room, and Risa thought Jodi resembled the abominable snow monster. She was covered with white, wet snow from head to toe.

"C'mon, Kiddo, let's get that snowsuit off."

The house seemed to shrink in size as the sound of children's voices filled it. The older Kreske kids piled into the bathroom to wash up, while David helped the two younger ones at the kitchen sink.

"Well, everything's all ready," Patti said, carrying the roast into the dining room. "Let's eat!"

twelve

"The meal was delicious," Risa told Patti from her place at the table. "Thanks."

"You're quite welcome."

"Your cake isn't bad, either, Risa," David declared, holding a forkful. "Want to come over every Sunday? You and my wife make a great team."

Risa smiled. "I'm glad you think so."

"I heard you're a terrific cook," Mike said, looking at her askance while finishing his dessert.

"I don't know about terrific," Risa replied, "but I'm not half bad. And I enjoy cooking and baking, so I'm always looking for people to feed."

"Bring it over here whenever you like," David said.

"Oh, as if you don't get enough to eat." Patti rolled her eyes.

"I'm only being hospitable, Hon."

Mike chuckled, and Risa's smile grew.

"Tell you what—you can feed me anytime, Risa," Mike said, turning toward her with a spark of mischief in his cocoa-colored eyes.

"I'll keep that in mind," she shot back.

Patti grinned, sending Risa a knowing look. Then she stood and began clearing the table. Risa glanced around Mike and found that Jodi had fallen asleep in the family room while watching a video with the other children.

Returning her gaze to her hostess, Risa decided to help. She rose, but Mike caught her wrist.

"How 'bout we sit in the living room for awhile?"

She hesitated, not wanting to leave Mike's sister with a mess to clean up alone.

"Go on, Risa," David said, as if sensing her inner dilemma. "Patti and I will take care of the dishes."

"Well, if you're sure. . ."

"He's sure." Mike released her wrist before standing. Then with a glance at Risa and a nod toward the front room, he added, "Let's go."

"All right. Lead the way."

Following Mike through the house, Risa's curiosity resurfaced. How could she possibly be someone Leslie Owens could use as a threat against Mike? Furthermore, why would Leslie threaten him at all?

No sooner had Risa stepped into the living room, when she voiced those very questions.

"Aw, Risa, it's a long story," Mike said with a long sigh as he led her to the floral-upholstered settee. "Remember that night in the parking lot?" he asked with a little wince.

"The night you kissed me? Sure, I remember." She smiled. "You can kiss me again if you want."

Mike laughed. "And wouldn't I love to. . ."

Risa regarded him, wondering at his reluctance. "It's okay, Mike."

"No, no. . .it's not. You see, Leslie saw me kiss you that night."

"So?"

"So, I'm a pastor, and I'm supposed to be aboveboard. Blameless."

"It was a kiss. Big deal." Risa frowned. "And what was Leslie doing downtown at that hour anyhow? Coming home from the bar?"

Mike didn't even grin at her sarcastic comeback. "No, she had gone to the all-night drugstore for some cold and flu medicine."

"A likely story."

Mike shook his head. "Leslie is a godly woman. I have no reason to doubt her. But I do have to apologize to you, Risa.

I never should have taken such liberties."

"Liberties?" She laughed. "I hardly call a kiss taking liberties."

"Well, that's what I call it, and I'm famous for preaching purity to our youth group."

"They're teenagers, Mike. We're adults. Besides, I hardly think a kiss makes for impurity."

"Perhaps, but I'm supposed to set an example."

Risa shook her head at him. "You're beating yourself up over nothing. But if it makes you feel better, I accept your apology."

"Thank you."

She thought it over and a million questions flitted through her mind. "So, if a pastor gets married, can he—"

"That's different. Intimacy between a man and his wife is a gift from God."

"Well, that's good." Risa pursed her lips, still pensive. "Are there a lot of rules for Christians? I mean, can I get a list or something so I know what I should or shouldn't be doing?"

Mike chuckled, but his expression wasn't mocking, it was tender.

"There's no list. There's the Bible. That's our 'rule book.' God convicts us through our consciences too. For instance, if you walked into a store and felt tempted to steal a pair of shoes, your conscience would tell you that it's wrong to steal and that you shouldn't do it. Being the good citizen that you are, you would listen to your conscience and decide not to take what didn't belong to you. That's the same way God's Holy Spirit works in a believer's life. When the believer is about to do something, that still, small voice alerts him to whether it's right or wrong. The problem is, a lot of Christians ignore God's tug at their heartstrings. . .like I did the night I kissed you."

Risa felt a little hurt, mostly because she'd enjoyed their kiss and still didn't really see why it was "wrong." However, if Mike said it was, who was she to question him?

"Can I ask you something personal?" Mike asked softly.

She shrugged.

"I'll take that as a yes." He smiled. "Are you a Christian, Risa?"

"Yes, so you can stop hounding me," she replied flippantly.

"Hounding you?" Mike dramatically placed his right hand over his heart. "I'm wounded."

"Oh, no, you're not. You wanted to see me converted, so now I am."

Mike's face split into a wide grin. "Oh, yeah? When did this happen?"

"On the morning after Kari died. I gave my soul to God, and. . ." She laughed. "Ironically, it was Leslie Owens who prompted me to do it."

"She prayed with you?"

"No. She said I should give God all my hurt and pain, and I replied, 'Don't you have to give your soul to Him first?' Then Leslie said something like, 'Yes, but who else would you give it to?' I thought it over and couldn't think of who else I would give my soul to. I sure don't want the devil to have it."

"Amen!" Mike exclaimed.

"And that's it." Risa frowned. "I think that's it. . .isn't it?"

"Only God knows your heart."

Risa nodded. "Then that *was* it. I mean, Wren had shown me verses in the Bible, I'd heard it from you, from your church. . .even from Kari when she read me that tract Mary Beth gave her. But I didn't understand. . .until Leslie said something so simple. Then everything sort of clicked."

"That's great!" Mike was all smiles. "So you got saved while we were in Italy?"

"I guess so." Risa was pretty sure, anyway. She shifted and crossed her leg. "And now, paradoxically, it's Leslie who's threatening you, hmm?"

Mike heaved a heavy sigh and nodded. "She said that unless I make a public confession, she's going to talk to

Kevin and the deacons about terminating my position."

"Over a kiss?" Risa shook her head. "That's her jealousy talking; you know that, right? You can't possibly be so naive that you don't see it, Mike. Leslie is jealous. Had you kissed her, it wouldn't be a federal offense."

Mike stretched his arm across the back of the settee, tempting Risa to scoot over closer to him. But just as he'd said, a subtle little inner nudge, a prompting, told her to stay right where she was.

At that very moment, Risa knew beyond a shadow of a doubt that she was really a Christian.

"I think jealousy is a part of it. . . . Yes, I would agree," Mike said. "But I was wrong."

Risa tossed a glance heavenward. "Whatever."

"On the other hand, this really isn't as bad as Leslie has made it seem. Even to me."

"How's that?" She turned to look at him.

"Well, the way Leslie tells the story, I was out carousing until the wee hours of the morning with an unsaved woman who's leading me down the wrong path. But the truth is, I spent a lovely evening at my cousin's restaurant with a sweet Christian lady."

"I thought you were out with me," Risa teased.

"I meant you," Mike replied, looking troubled.

She laughed. "I know. I'm kidding."

He answered with an abashed grin.

"Mike, you have to understand. Sweet and Christian have never, ever, been words that described me. Now, tramp and hussy. . .they were a couple of my stepfather's favorites."

Mike shook his head. "I'm sorry to hear that. I can't imagine a father ever speaking to his daughter that way."

"Yeah, well, you'll be even sorrier to hear that they were true, at least as far as Christians are concerned!"

"Risa, don't." He placed his hand on her shoulder. "Everyone's a sinner. 'There is none righteous, no, not one.' It doesn't matter what kind of sin; sin is sin. But because of Christ, you've been born again, birthed in His righteousness. Old things pass away. From here on in, everything is new. You're a child of the King."

"Guess that makes me a princess, huh?" She smiled, finding it still so hard to fathom. She never thought the day would come when she'd be a born-again Christian.

"Princess Risa," Mike teased.

Her smile broadened. "So, what are you going to do about Leslie?"

"I'm going to pray, then talk to Kevin before I *do* anything."

"That's probably wise."

Several amicable moments of silence passed between them, and then Mike laughed.

Risa looked his way, curious.

"Can I ask you another personal question?"

"I guess so."

"You can tell me if I'm out of line."

She grinned. "I will. Don't worry."

Mike chuckled, but then paused as if in deliberation. "Did, um. . ."

"Yes?"

"I mean, it really doesn't matter to me one way or another. . . ."

She arched a brow and could only imagine what he wanted to ask. "I haven't exactly lived like a nun, if that's what you're wanting to know."

The poor man actually blushed. "No, no. . .I would never ask such a thing." He cleared his throat.

"I didn't mean to embarrass you, but to a lot of guys, that's important. I just thought with you being a pastor—"

"No, no. . ."

Mike cleared his throat again, and Risa felt sorry for him. Moreover, she got the distinct feeling his past reputation as "Madman Mike" would pale in comparison to hers. But she took comfort in knowing that, like he said, "old things passed away, all things were new."

Standing, she walked from the settee to the window and looked over the snow-covered lawn. Then she pivoted abruptly. "Spit it out, Mike. What do you want to know?"

He sat forward, his hands folded over his knees. Raising his chin, he gave her an intent look. "Did Wren ever kiss you?"

Risa almost laughed at him for asking such a stupid thing. "No, he never kissed me, but I tried every trick in the book to remedy that. Didn't work, though."

Mike stood and walked slowly toward her, wearing an earnest expression. "Forgive me for asking, but I keep wondering if you still have feelings for him."

"Feelings? Well, sure I do. But 'feelings' covers a gamut of emotions, don't you think?"

Mike nodded solemnly.

"But I'm not in love with him, if that's what you're getting at."

"Yeah, that's what I was getting at."

Risa shook her head. "A relationship between Wren and me was never meant to be. I see that now. I even saw that then, but I pretended I didn't. Wren never led me on. I always knew where he stood. He was a Christian, I wasn't, and there's a rule about not getting romantically involved with someone who's not born again."

"It's called being unequally yoked."

"Yeah, that sounds familiar."

Mike grinned, his expression both tender and amused.

"What's more," Risa continued, "Wren loved his ex-wife—now his wife again—and I thought he was nuts. But he held out and got what he wanted, and in all honesty, I'm happy for him."

Mike stepped closer and leaned against the wall. He glanced down at the toes of his black dress shoes. "Thanks for sharing that with me." He looked up at her at last. "Now can I ask something else?"

Her first impulse was to give him a sarcastic retort. But again, that little nudge inside told her this was serious. "Sure, Mike. What is it?"

He pursed his lips momentarily, then wetted them. In every sense, Risa thought he looked nervous. Was he going to propose or something?

She held her breath, hoping that wasn't the case. Like Wren, she had feelings for Mike, but she hadn't decided what they were yet.

"Do you think a. . .a relationship between us is 'meant to be'?"

Risa swallowed hard. He looked like a boy, baring his soul. "Maybe."

He blinked, obviously not thrilled with her reply. Shifting his gaze to the view beyond the window, he said, "I, um. . ." He chuckled in self-reproach, then looked back at her. "I think I've been in love with you since the first day I met you at the gym. It was a year ago, and you were sitting in the bleachers with Wren's girls, remember? Nancie came in later, and the two of you had a spat. . . ."

"I remember," she murmured. However, Risa's heart was still banging from Mike's admission. He loved her? Her next thought was, *He probably shouldn't.*

"Mike, you're really sweet," she began carefully, "but if I'm not mistaken, you're implying something permanent."

He nodded. "I am."

"Well, I don't think I'd make a good pastor's wife."

"Why not?"

Because I'm not in love with the pastor, she wanted to say. However, she couldn't hurt him by being so blunt.

"Mike, I know nothing about being a born-again Christian."

"It's all in the Bible, and you'll soon learn it."

Hardheaded Italian, Risa thought. She probably would have to be brusque in order to get the message through his thick skull.

But then she suddenly thought of the perfect answer. She donned a sober expression. "We should pray about this."

Mike smiled. "I agree."

Disappointment assailed her. She hadn't meant it as a positive thing. Risa was a bit afraid of prayer, equating it to waking a sleeping giant. Why bother God with such a mundane issue? He might not appreciate it.

"Risa, that's all I ask. . .that you pray about it. About us."

She tried not to wince. "Okay." It was an act of passive resistance, because she already knew the answer. No!

She would never marry Mike Gerardi. She'd never be a pastor's wife.

thirteen

After Risa agreed to pray about their relationship, Mike was so delighted, he felt as though he were walking with his head in the clouds. This was true to the extent that he barely noticed his disappointment when, later, Risa announced she wouldn't go back to church for the evening service. She said her feet hurt and that she had a long day ahead of her tomorrow.

"Yeah, but Risa," Patti said, "you'll have it worse at home with Jodi, since she slept all afternoon. You'll have to entertain her until at least eight-thirty. Why don't you come back to church, where you can sit and relax, rest your aching feet, while Jodi plays in the nursery?"

Mike watched Risa nibble her lower lip in indecision.

"C'mon," Patti cajoled. "You just got done saying your apartment isn't geared for a two year old. The nurseries at church are."

"Oh, all right. You've got a point. I'll go back to church with you guys."

Mike grinned.

"You're as bad as your brother," Risa told her, sending Mike a pointed stare. "Now I know where he gets it."

He laughed, feeling oddly flattered over the implication that he could influence Risa. He knew only too well that she wasn't a woman easily persuaded.

A little more than an hour later, Mike left her in the company of his sister and strolled down the church's corridor. As he headed for his office, he passed Kevin's and paused in the doorway. As usual, the senior pastor's office was cluttered with books and papers, but Mike had to marvel at the man. Kevin Batzler had an organized mess and knew where everything

107

was, right down to paper clips and pens.

"Hey, Kev, I've got to talk with you."

"Yeah, I've got to talk with you too," Kevin said, looking up from the paper in his hand. "Come on in."

Mike stepped forward and closed the door behind him. He guessed what was coming, but he hadn't planned to have this conversation until tomorrow.

"Leslie Owens phoned me this afternoon."

"I figured that when you said you wanted to talk to me. I spoke with Leslie earlier."

"Yeah, that's what she said."

Putting his hands on his hips, Mike shook his head. "I promised her I would speak with you, but I see that wasn't good enough."

"She said she had to 'unburden' herself because she's been holding all this in for two weeks."

"Well, good, I hope she feels better now."

A hint of a grin tugged at Kevin's mouth. "So let's hear your side of the story."

Mike drew in a breath. "It's the same. Leslie isn't lying and I won't deny her accusation. It's true. I kissed Risa. I knew I did wrong after it happened, and I know it now, but I can't undo what's been done. I have, however, mentioned this to Risa and explained why I shouldn't have kissed her. I don't think she agrees, but I believe she understands."

"Why would she agree if she's not a Christian? I'm sure this whole thing sounds ludicrous to someone like her."

"Risa *is* a Christian. She accepted Christ in Italy, and I've heard her testimony. Furthermore, I've seen the change in her."

Kevin sighed. "Well, that's a relief. Leslie made it sound like you were habitually gallivanting till dawn, living like the world, and dating an unbeliever."

"Great." Mike rubbed his jaw, thinking over the situation. "Risa said Leslie is jealous."

"Julie said the same thing, and I thought about it. There

might be some truth to it. But we're still going to have to deal with this situation somehow and in a way that satisfies even Leslie. I mean, something of this nature could bring trouble to our church, and our ministry could suffer." Kevin tilted his head. "Any bright ideas?"

Mike grinned. "Lemme sleep on it."

"Sure." Kevin looked a bit skeptical. "We'll talk more tomorrow."

"Right." Mike turned to go.

"Oh, and, um. . ."

Mike wheeled back around. "Yes?"

"Just what exactly are your intentions concerning this woman. . .Risa?"

Seeing no point in beating around the bush, Mike spoke his mind. "I love her and I plan to marry her."

Kevin snorted. "Yeah, I thought that might be what you were thinking."

"Risa has agreed to pray about it. . .about us. Talk about miraculous."

"Can't deny that." Kevin sobered. "Just be careful, Mike. After I fell in love with Julie I couldn't see straight, let alone be practical where she was concerned. It was like my common sense flew right out the window. I'll be eternally grateful to my wife for having suggested a short engagement."

Mike nodded and grinned. "I hear you."

"Good."

Feeling properly chastened, Mike left Kevin's office, strode purposefully several feet down the hallway, and entered his own office. In contrast to Kevin's "home away from home," as he sometimes referred to his office here at church, Mike's was tidy. He kept up with his filing, so the top of his desk was void of paperwork and clutter. Mike's small library of books was neatly arranged in the bookshelf he'd purchased and put together. The mock-mahogany unit now stood in the far corner of his office.

Mike checked his voice mail, gathered his Bible and day planner, then made his way back to the sanctuary. Entering, he halted when he saw Risa sitting in a pew with four teenage girls hovering around her. It appeared that they were discussing music CDs, given the flat, square case Risa held in her hands.

They like her, Mike noted. *And why not? An attractive, outgoing woman like Risa. . .what teenage girl wouldn't want to be like her when she grew up?* Risa had a professional bearing, but no one had to wonder where he stood with her. Perhaps that's what drew Mary Beth, Tracy, and the other two teens sitting by her—Risa's transparency. She didn't put on airs like some adults. She was simply Risa.

Mike sauntered over to the little huddle. "Hey, whassup?" he drawled.

The girls greeted him with cordial smiles, while Risa explained how she was being educated on Christian music.

"I guess I never knew such a thing existed," she added. "I mean, I've heard of gospel music, but. . ."

"Well, you'll like this," Tracy assured her, tapping her finger on one particular CD. "It's instrumental, and it's totally relaxing."

"Great. Thanks for letting me borrow it," Risa replied.

Mike stood by, grinning, and then a lively duet filled the air. He swung his gaze to the front and noticed one of Bay Community Church's faithful members at the organ while Leslie Owens sat at the piano's keyboard. Mike felt his grin slip and anger well in his gut, but he knew he couldn't afford to let bitterness take root. He told himself Leslie wasn't acting out of malice but out of concern.

Now he just had to believe it.

"We'd better get to choir," one of the girls said. "We're singing tonight, and you know how nervous Mr. Pippins gets if we're not in the choir room on time."

"Now, there's a dude who needs to learn how to relax," Mary Beth retorted.

The four bid Risa good-bye, and Mike felt a little hurt that they all but ignored him when they departed.

"You're a hit," he told Risa as he took a seat next to her.

She smiled. "They're nice girls."

"Sure are." He glanced around the sanctuary. "Where are Patti and David?"

Risa shrugged. "Don't know, but they left their stuff here. See?"

Mike leaned forward and saw four Bibles resting on the pew. His two younger nephews would be in the nursery tonight, but Delaney and Peter would sit beside their parents.

"Leslie called Kevin this afternoon," Mike stated softly so that no one could overhear. "I just came from discussing the situation with him."

He watched as Risa's gaze shifted toward the piano. "Are you in trouble?"

"No, but Kevin wants me to come up with some sort of remedy that will appease everyone involved."

"Hmm. . ." Risa appeared to think it over, then turned toward him. "I've got it. Why don't you preach next Sunday on temptation? You can incorporate what happened in your sermon and then blame it all on me. Tell everyone I tempted you just like Eve tempted Adam. Then you can end by saying how weak men are." She laughed.

"Thanks, Risa," Mike replied dryly. "I knew I could count on you."

She laughed once more, a bit louder this time, and Mike saw Leslie glance in their direction. He purposely avoided making eye contact with her.

"Sorry to be such a smart aleck," Risa said, "but I read about Adam and Eve in the Garden a few nights ago. Aren't you impressed?"

Mike looked into her upturned face and smiled. "Sure am." A moment later, he forced himself to look away, although he realized he'd like nothing better than to gaze into Risa's eyes for the rest of his life. However, he was in enough hot water for the time being.

He mulled over the situation, and the more he thought about Risa's suggestion, the more he decided a modified version might just work.

"You know, I think I'll take your advice after all," Mike said, still pensive. "I'll ask Kevin if I can preach next Sunday on temptation, and—"

"Well, don't expect *me* to show up."

"Not to worry. I have no intention of mentioning your name." He grinned. "I won't even allude to your gorgeous red hair."

She rewarded him with a pretty blush. "I was being facetious about the sermon thing, Mike."

"I know, but it might work. I'll pray about it and see what I can come up with."

"Fine, but I think I'm going to have a headache next Sunday morning."

"No, you won't." With that, Mike stood and walked to the front of the church, where he met Kevin, who was on his way to the podium.

fourteen

Thunder woke Risa on Monday morning, fifteen minutes before her alarm was set to go off. She wanted to roll over and go back to sleep, but she remembered that she needed to drive out to Brookfield and drop Jodi off at her cousin's house.

Risa suddenly became aware of the small body nestled beside her. The little stinker had pitched a fit the last two nights, refusing to sleep in the portable crib Risa purchased. Instead, Jodi insisted she "go night-night in big bed." Risa couldn't see any harm in it, and besides, the poor kid was probably feeling insecure after her mother went away and never came back.

Risa's eyes filled with unshed tears. She missed Kari, and it wasn't easy to forget her when she had Jodi around.

Propping herself up on her elbow, Risa leaned over and kissed Jodi's down-soft blond hair. Then she crawled out of bed, careful not to awaken the little girl. She padded to the window, pulled back the ivory lace curtains, and looked outside. The black sky brightened only when a jagged lightning bolt ripped through its dark veil. A roll of thunder followed. This was one of those odd winter storms whose rain would likely turn to sleet and snow as the day wore on.

"Are you angry, God?" Risa whispered, looking as far upward as she could see. "I went to church yesterday," she reminded Him. "I went *twice!* That should make You happy." She sighed, watching the rain fall. She wondered if maybe God were crying—sobbing, in fact. Maybe He peered down from heaven and saw Jodi, virtually an orphan at age two, and one who got shuffled like a deck of cards. That would make anyone weep.

Wiping a tear from her eye, Risa gave herself a mental shake. She had always possessed an overactive imagination, which explained why she enjoyed writing. Lately, however, she hadn't had the time or inclination to sit down and create a story.

Risa continued in the prayerful vein, but on a more realistic note this time. "Traffic is going to be horrendous, and I've got to drive out of my way this morning. Please, Jesus, will You stop the rain. . .at least until I get to work?"

Letting the curtain fall back into place, Risa figured she was being selfish. There were probably people who had prayed for rain. How did God decide which prayers to answer, who to please, and who to disappoint? Risa stepped into the shower, deciding that God had a tough job.

She shampooed her hair, washed up, then turned off the water and towel-dried herself. Back in the bedroom, she noticed Jodi was still sound asleep. Clad in her bathrobe, Risa walked to the kitchen and prepared coffee. Thinking over her morning routine, she elected to get herself ready before waking Jodi.

On a typical day, Risa left for work at eight-fifteen. That gave her plenty of time to get downtown, park, and walk to her office by nine. But today Risa walked out of her apartment at six-fifteen, since it was forty-five minutes out to Brookfield and forty-five back.

Carrying Jodi to the car, a diaper bag slung over her shoulder, she suddenly noticed the rain had stopped.

"Thank You, Jesus," she said, strapping Jodi into her car seat.

"Fank You, Yesus," Jodi mimicked.

"Rain, rain go away. Come again some other day."

Jodi giggled.

Smiling at the child, Risa closed the back door. Then she climbed in behind the wheel, started her car, and drove off.

❧

It was Wednesday, and Mike hadn't been able to make contact

with Risa. Sitting behind his desk, he stared at the phone, wondering why she hadn't returned any of his calls.

She had her hands full—he knew that. She said she had volunteered to watch Jodi this week, and she worked a full-time job besides.

I shouldn't be so impatient, Father, he prayed. *I have to remember, not my will, but Thine.*

Turning back to his computer and the database he'd been assigned to update, Mike did his best to push thoughts of a certain hazel-eyed redhead from his mind.

❧

Risa walked out of South Bend Mutual Life at five-thirty, relieved that Friday evening had finally come. She found her car in the underground lot and drove out to Brookfield to fetch Jodi. It was time for the little one to go back to her grandmother's house. After dropping her off, Risa would then race to the bridal shop to meet Annamarie. Tonight's agenda consisted of making the final selection on the bridesmaids' gowns.

Reaching Therese's house, Risa collected Jodi and all the paraphernalia that went along with a two year old.

"Thanks so much for watching her," Risa said, giving her cousin's wife a hug. "I don't know how I would have survived without you this week."

"Hey, no sweat," Therese replied. When the sisterly embrace ended, she stepped back and finger-combed her short, brown hair off her forehead. "Jodi's an angel."

Risa turned and smiled at the little girl who sat strapped into her car seat, all ready for the ride to Kari's mother's house. "I love her," she said, "but kids are a handful. I haven't had a minute to myself all week."

"I can relate," Therese replied. "But I must confess that I looked forward to your cooking every night. It was awesome not to have to make dinner. That was a break for me, Risa."

"Well, it's the least I could do."

She walked around to the driver's side of the car and crawled in. Starting the engine, she waved good-bye to Therese before accelerating down the quiet, suburban street.

On the way to Arlene's, she pondered all the tasks awaiting her this weekend. She had to phone Mike; the poor guy had left three messages. Laundry needed to be done, groceries bought, and, of course, tonight was shot, what with helping Annamarie shop for dresses. Risa felt exhausted just thinking over her to-do list.

"Oh, yeah, and church on Sunday," she muttered, wondering how she'd ever accomplish anything this weekend.

An hour later, after getting stuck in the last of rush-hour traffic, Risa pulled alongside the curb in front of Arlene's. The house Kari's mother rented was the lowerhalf of an old duplex whose wooden siding had seen better days.

Helping Jodi up the rickety porch stairs, Risa rang the front doorbell. Moments later, Arlene flung open the door and, holding the portable phone to her ear, she waved Risa in with her free hand.

Never a "hello" or even a smile to her granddaughter, Risa noted. She felt somewhat rankled; little Jodi deserved a better welcome than that. Nana still met her at the door and cupped Risa's face, kissing her like she was eleven.

Furthermore, Arlene didn't offer to help carry in any of Jodi's belongings.

But finally after three trips, Risa had made a neat little pile in Arlene's living room. She was only too glad she'd removed her heels and replaced them with white bobby socks and comfy athletic shoes before leaving the office.

Glancing into the connecting dining room now, Risa saw the older woman still on the phone and smoking a cigarette. "Sorry, but I've got to leave," she said, trying to interrupt as politely as possible.

Again, Arlene just waved.

Figuring that's the best "thanks" she'd get, Risa hunkered

in front of Jodi. "Bye, Honey. I'll see you soon, okay?"

The little girl frowned.

"I love you." Risa pulled her close and kissed her velvety cheek. Standing, she then strode to the door, hearing Jodi begin to cry. She felt terrible, but told herself that Jodi would be fine in a few minutes.

However, the next thing she knew, the child had wrapped herself around her legs, and Risa nearly tripped onto the porch.

"Honey, I have to go bye-bye. You stay with Grandma."

"Nooooo!" she wailed.

Risa glanced at Arlene, whom she could see still sitting at the dining-room table. "Excuse me," she called, "but could you help me out here?"

Arlene set the phone down, looking irritated.

Meanwhile, Jodi's small fists were fastened onto Risa's navy blue skirt. "Honey, you stay with your grandma."

"No, no, no. . ."

Arlene stuck her cigarette in her mouth and peeled the little girl's fingers from Risa's clothing. "Get in the house and be quiet," she muttered, depositing her granddaughter in the tiny foyer and then giving her bottom a swat.

Straightening, she removed her cigarette and smiled. "Thanks, and see you later."

The door closed.

As she stood motionless on the front porch, Risa could hear Jodi screaming inside.

"Wisa, Wisa," she cried, and moments later, Risa could hear Jodi banging on the door. "Wisa. . ."

Next, Risa heard Arlene holler, "Shut up and sit down."

Risa put her face in her hands. *Oh, God, I can't leave her here.* Despairing, she glanced heavenward, all the while listening to Jodi's hysterics behind the door. She'd been fine at Therese's all week, fine in the nursery last Sunday. . . .

With a sigh, Risa pressed on the bell.

Arlene opened the door, wearing a scowl. "Now what?"

Risa swallowed down her frustration while Jodi wiggled her way around her grandmother only to cling to Risa again. "I can keep her awhile longer," she said. "If it's okay with you."

Arlene rolled her eyes and walked away. "I don't care."

Lifting Jodi, she held the child close, soothing her. "It's all right, Sweetie. You can come home with me, okay?"

The death grip around Risa's neck was answer enough.

So with a two year old fastened to her hip, Risa began making trips to the car, repacking the trunk and half of the backseat. Once again, Arlene didn't lift a finger to help, and by the time she'd set Jodi in her car seat, Risa was livid. It took every ounce of self-control she had to keep from blasting the older woman with a piece of her mind. The only thing that kept her from doing so was the fear that Arlene wouldn't allow her to take Jodi.

Well, I shouldn't be surprised, Risa fumed as she drove to the bridal shop on the north end of town. She recalled Kari's tearful accounts of her mother's lack of interest in her or Jodi. Then, after José's rejection, Kari said she felt so alone. That's when Risa had tried to help out some. She let Jodi sleep overnight on several occasions so Kari could go out or just have time to herself. After this past week, Risa understood why Kari had coveted such opportunities. However, as tired as she felt, Risa wasn't about to leave Jodi with Arlene.

But I can't keep her forever. What do I do?

Before she could really dwell on the question, Risa reached the bridal shop and found a parking spot. Then, after unfastening Jodi, she prayed that Annamarie wouldn't be angry that a two year old was tagging along.

"But I guess the first thing we have to do is feed you, huh?" Risa said, giving Jodi a quick smooch before setting her down.

Taking the child's hand, Risa led her to the front of the store, where her cousin stood wide-eyed with curiosity, waiting for her.

fifteen

By Friday night, Mike had become downright concerned. He had reached the conclusion Risa wouldn't ignore him. If she didn't want to talk to him for whatever reason, she'd tell him point blank first. Therefore, something kept her from returning his phone calls, and he decided he needed to find out what that "something" could be.

"Hey, Claudio," he called to his cousin who lounged on the couch, paging through a sports magazine, "how 'bout coming with me to pay Risa a visit?"

"Risa?"

"*Si.* She's the woman I told you about."

Claudio still wore a confused expression.

"*Mi amore*," Mike said in Italian, hoping he'd gotten the words correct. He grinned sheepishly and placed a dramatic hand over his heart. "My love."

Claudio nodded and grinned. "*Si.*"

"I want to visit her. Will you come with me?"

"Me?"

"*Si. Chaperone.*"

Claudio sat up and laughed, giving his knee a slap. "Oh, okay, chaperone. Okay." He laughed again.

As they left his apartment, Mike felt somewhat insulted by his cousin's mirth; however, he soon realized that not many men his age asked for a chaperone. Mike, on the other hand, figured bringing Claudio along was the best way to keep temptation at bay. He planned to incorporate that simple solution into his message Sunday morning too.

❧

Risa could barely keep her eyes open as she drove home

119

from the bridal shop. After a supper of hamburgers and French fries, both Jodi's favorites, Risa and Annamarie had poured over one catalog after another. Risa even tried on a couple of bridesmaid gowns just for fun. But now it was nearly ten o'clock, and Jodi had fallen asleep in her car seat, having put in a full day for a two year old.

Risa yawned. She'd put in a full day herself!

Finding a parking place in front of her apartment building, Risa pulled the car alongside the curb. She killed the engine, collected her purse, and climbed out of the car. Opening the back door, she eased Jodi from her car seat, careful not to wake her. The little girl's head flopped onto Risa's shoulder, and her snowsuit-encased arms dangled around Risa's neck. But sleeping, Jodi was dead weight, and Risa knew she couldn't carry anything more. She'd have to wait until tomorrow to haul Jodi's belongings from her car's trunk up to her apartment.

"Risa!"

She turned and squinted into the darkness at the two men striding in her direction. It didn't take but a moment to recognize Mike. The other guy, however, she didn't know.

"Hey, I've been worried about you," Mike said when he finally stood a few feet away.

"I've had a hectic week," she replied. "I'm sorry I didn't get a chance to return your calls."

"That's okay, but, like I said, I got concerned."

"Thanks." Risa glanced at the other man, and Mike quickly made the introductions.

"This is my cousin Claudio. Claudio, meet Risa Vitalis."

The man nodded politely. "Good pleasure."

She smiled and looked back at Mike. "No *comprensione* English, eh?"

"Little bit," Claudio said in his defense.

Mike gave his cousin a friendly clap on the back. "With my 'little bit' of Italian and his 'little bit' of English, we manage."

"I'm sure." Risa shifted Jodi's weight, feeling like her arms were about to give way. "Would you two like to come up for a soda or something? I have to get Jodi to bed."

"Yeah, sure. Can we help you with anything?" Mike asked. "Want me to take Jodi for you?"

The trunk, which contained a portable crib, high chair, and bag of toys, and her backseat stuffed with Jodi's clothes and diapers, suddenly came to mind.

She popped the lid open with the button on her key chain. "You guys are a godsend. I'd love some help."

The two men gathered the items, which didn't seem like much of a load for them to carry. But Risa sighed with relief all the way up to the second floor.

"I can't thank you two enough," she said as they entered her apartment. "You can set down all that stuff anywhere. Then make yourselves at home while I put Jodi in bed."

"Will do," Mike replied.

In her bedroom, Risa lay the child down on the bed. Next, she hustled back into the living room to fetch a nightie and a diaper. "I've got some soda in the fridge," she offered.

"We're okay, Risa."

Claudio nodded, looking a tad confused.

Back in her room, she smiled sympathetically. Risa knew the feeling of being in a country where you can't understand the language well—especially if someone spoke too fast.

Risa changed Jodi, who woke up, looked around, glanced at Risa, and smiled sleepily. Then all by herself, she crawled into the "big bed" and pulled the covers around her little body. She was sleeping again by the time Risa had gotten her dirty clothes into the hamper.

"Jodi's exhausted, poor thing." Risa collapsed into one of the stuffed, geometrical-print armchairs, while both men sat on her burgundy leather sofa. "Are you sure I can't get you anything?"

Mike waved away the offer.

"Nice–a place," Claudio said.

"*Grazie*." Risa looked back at Mike. "You wouldn't believe what happened tonight when I tried to drop off Jodi at her grandmother's house."

"What?" Mike sat back and propped his right foot on his left knee.

"Well, first, Arlene didn't exactly give us a warm welcome. Then Jodi pitched one of her temper fits because she didn't want me to leave. That made Arlene mad, so she started yelling at Jodi. I couldn't stand to leave her there, so I offered to take care of her. . .indefinitely, I suppose."

"Are you going to be able to do that?" Mike said, his dark brows furrowed with concern.

Risa sighed. "I don't know."

Claudio tapped Mike on the shoulder, asking something in Italian. Mike scratched his head.

"What iz this?" Claudio tried again, pointing to Risa, then at his cousin. "Why Risa sad?"

"Oh!" Mike nodded, then turned and gave Risa a grin. "He wants to know what we're talking about."

Risa shrugged. "I'm sure it seems like we're being rude and leaving him out of the conversation."

For the next several minutes, Mike and Risa did their best to explain who Jodi was and what had happened tonight. It finally became something akin to a game of charades, which got Risa laughing. But at last Claudio understood—either that or he didn't care anymore.

"Hey, since you have Jodi this weekend," Mike suggested, "why don't we go to the museum tomorrow?"

Risa shook her head. "I've got too much to do."

"Like what?"

"Like wash clothes, pick up a couple of my skirts from the dry cleaners, grocery shop. . . ."

"I can help with the latter two. I'll stop at the cleaners on my way and get your stuff. We'll go to the museum and then stop for groceries on the way back. By then Jodi will be sufficiently exhausted and you can do your laundry."

Risa pursed her lips, thinking it over. She couldn't deny that having an extra pair of hands around would make caring for Jodi and getting her tasks done much easier. "Okay. Sounds good." She gave him a skeptical look. "You really don't mind stopping at the dry cleaners for me?"

"Not at all."

"Great. I'll go find my claim ticket."

In her room, she scooped up her purse and brought it back into the living room near the light. She scrounged around in her wallet until she finally found the small voucher.

Meanwhile, Mike and Claudio had stood and appeared ready to leave. Handing Mike the ticket, Risa gave him the name of the dry cleaners as well.

"I really appreciate this."

"No problem. What are friends for, eh?" Mike motioned Claudio to the door before turning to give Risa a little wink. "How does noon sound?"

"Sounds good." She smiled, watching him go and thinking there wasn't a nicer guy in the world than Mike Gerardi.

sixteen

Risa had just finished wiping sticky pancake syrup off of Jodi's hands when the intercom buzzed, announcing a visitor in the downstairs lobby. Glancing at the kitchen clock, Risa didn't think it could be Mike at this early hour. Nine-thirty? He'd promised to give her until noon! Another buzz of the intercom and, after settling Jodi in front of some cartoons, Risa answered the call.

"Good morning," came the female voice. "This is Leslie Owens. I'd like to speak with you if you can spare a few minutes."

Risa glanced down at the nightshirt she wore. She'd been planning to take a quick shower and dress, seeing as Jodi was fed and preoccupied for the time being. "Well, um. . ."

"It won't take long."

Risa sighed, wondering what the woman wanted. Did she plan to lecture her on the evils of kissing a pastor? If so, Risa had a few words of her own she'd like to share.

She pressed on the button, which allowed Leslie access into the building. In the interim, Risa found her robe and, pulling it on, she tied it at the waist. A knock on the door followed moments later.

"Hi," Leslie said with a tight smile. "Thanks for letting me speak with you."

"C'mon in," Risa replied, opening the door wider. "Can I take your coat?"

Nodding, Leslie shrugged out of the camel hair wool overcoat and handed it to Risa, who hung it in the closet. Then, in a sweeping glance, she noticed Leslie's baggy blue-and-white-checked jumper, which covered the length of her tall, thin form, and she couldn't help but think the woman looked somewhat frumpy.

Closing the door, Risa then became aware of Jodi's curious inspection of their guest.

"This is Leslie," Risa said. "Leslie, meet Jodi."

"Oh," Leslie exclaimed, seeing the two year old. "I didn't know you had children."

"I don't. This is Kari's little girl. . . . Kari, my friend who died in Italy. Remember?"

Leslie's expression immediately turned sympathetic. "Yes. Of course. I'm sorry. . . ."

Risa felt abashed for her terse reply. "Have a seat, Leslie," she said on a lighter note. "Would you like some coffee?"

"No, thanks."

Jodi took the next few minutes to show Leslie her love-worn blanket, favorite stuffed bear, and storybook. Leslie graciously marveled over each treasured item.

"Okay, that's enough show 'n' tell," Risa told the child at last. "You sit down and watch your cartoons. Leslie and I are going to have a talk."

Jodi obeyed, curling up on the sofa with her blanket, bear, and book.

Standing, Risa waved Leslie into the sunny kitchen, which was separated from the living room by a mere half-wall. "Why don't we sit in here?" she suggested, pouring herself a cup of coffee. "Are you sure you wouldn't like a cup?"

"No, I don't drink anything with caffeine," Leslie replied, sitting in one of the two kitchen chairs.

"Don't tell me drinking coffee is a sin. I love my coffee." Risa took a sip.

"As long as you don't love it more than Jesus, it's not a sin."

The remark gave Risa pause, because it struck her as very odd. *Love it more than Jesus?* She'd never considered such a thing.

"I actually came here to talk about Pastor Gerardi," Leslie

began, changing the subject, and Risa saw the faint blush that crept into the other woman's cheeks at the mention of Mike's name.

"I figured that. I mean, speaking of sin. . ." At Leslie's puzzled expression, she added, "I know you saw us kissing a few weeks ago."

If Leslie wasn't blushing before, she surely was now. In fact, she fairly glowed crimson.

"Look, Mike explained to me why it wasn't right and. . ." Risa sighed. "And I don't really understand, but I accept the reasoning, okay? It won't happen again, so I hope you'll stop blabbing it all over and making Mike look bad. He feels awful about it."

"Blabbing!" Leslie shook her head. "I'd never do such a thing."

"What are you talking about? You already have."

"I confronted Pastor Gerardi in a biblical manner and then told Pastor Batzler my concerns. That's all."

"Well, that's enough." Risa sipped her coffee, thinking Leslie looked frazzled. Then she shrugged. "Oh, whatever. Is that what you wanted to talk to me about?"

Leslie cleared her throat. "Um, sort of. . ." Looking down at her hands, primly folded on the tabletop, she seemed to grope for the right words. "I don't know how to say this, Miss Vitalis, but I worry that, perhaps, you're leading Pastor Gerardi down a path of destruction."

"Excuse me?" Risa felt horribly insulted.

"Oh, not intentionally, of course," Leslie amended, "but. . ." She looked up and her sky blue eyes met Risa's gaze. "But perhaps out of ignorance. You see, the kind of relationship our pastor is seeking to have with a woman is one that will result in marriage. I couldn't help wondering if you were aware of that."

"Yes, I am." Risa thought back to her discussion with Mike in the Kreskes' living room the previous Sunday. "We talked about it."

"And?"

"And. . .it's none of your business."

Leslie appeared to be taken aback by the crisp retort. "No, I suppose it isn't," she stated at last, "except that I care deeply about Pastor Gerardi and I want the best for him."

"And, of course, you think you're what's best," Risa said glibly.

"Well, no. . .I mean, I don't know that. How could I?"

Risa shrugged.

"At this point, I can only pray. On the other hand, I do understand what goes along with becoming a pastor's wife because my parents were in the ministry. Pastor Batzler said you're a Christian, and I'm glad to hear it, but are you ready for the duties that go along with the title of Mrs. Gerardi?"

An anxious knot tightened around Risa's heart. "What, exactly, is involved?"

"Various responsibilities, from making sure the church has been cleaned on Saturday night, to bake sales and cooking for church functions, to choosing Sunday school curriculum and counseling women in crisis."

Risa didn't think the list sounded too terribly difficult, except for maybe the latter two tasks. As far as handling life's crises, Risa regarded herself a pro. After all, she'd been through a lot and she hadn't lost her mind. . .yet.

"Being a pastor's wife also means dying to your own ambitions so your husband's ministry can succeed," Leslie continued. "It means learning to survive on meager wages but living abundantly in Christ and being an example to the rest of the congregation."

Risa surveyed the woman sitting at her kitchen counter, noting her simple appearance. Her plain but pretty face bore no cosmetics, and her clothing was unfashionable. As usual, her blond hair was pulled back into a tight coil, and somehow Risa couldn't believe Mike would want his wife to look so drab. Conversely, he was a dynamic guy. Furthermore, Risa had a hard time picturing Leslie at a lively Italian gathering.

Even so, one thing stood in the way of Risa ever becoming Mike's wife. . .the fact that she didn't love him.

Turning, she set down her coffee mug on the counter. "I'm not going to be a pastor's wife, so don't worry about it," she muttered.

"Then you're trying to persuade Pastor Gerardi to leave the ministry?"

Surprised, Risa spun around and faced Leslie again. "I'm not trying to persuade him to do anything."

"Maybe not in so many words, but with your actions. Like the night I saw the two of you—"

"Oh, give me a break! That kiss just happened. It wasn't something I conjured up in order to entice an unsuspecting pastor, if that's what you're implying. What's more, Mike started it. And for your information, I'm not leading him down a path of destruction, as you put it. For the first time in my life, I'm not even leading."

"Good. That's the way it should be," Leslie stated on a priggish note. "Relationships don't stand a chance unless it's the Lord who brings a man and a woman together."

Risa cocked a brow. "How do you know that God isn't bringing Mike and me together?"

Leslie turned momentarily pensive. "I guess I know because over the past year I've prayed about it, and I believe the Lord has called me to be a pastor's wife. Furthermore, I'm certain the pastor I'm to marry is Mike Gerardi."

Risa bit the inside of her cheek in an effort not to grin. "Well, God better inform Mike of that, because I don't think he has a clue."

Leslie obviously didn't find the quip the least bit funny. "I think God has been telling Mike, but he's not listening because. . .because you're in the way."

The reply stung like a slap; however, it forced Risa to recall the many times in her life when she felt the same frustration, only it was another woman "in the way." She'd come right out and told Nancie Nickelson to get out of Wren's life. Oh, what she wouldn't have given for Nancie to stay out of the way for a few weeks or a month—although it probably wouldn't have made a difference.

With arms akimbo, Risa stared hard at her latest opponent. Except, the situation was so skewed that she almost had to laugh. She didn't love Mike, so why not give Leslie a chance at him?

"Okay, tell you what. I'll get out of your way. . . ."

"God's way," Leslie corrected.

"All right, I'll get out of God's way, although I suspect He could get me out of the way all by Himself. But I'll step aside. In fact, I'll help you attract Mike's attention. We'll do something with your hair, buy a few different outfits, get you a makeover at the department store—"

"I could never do such a wanton thing!" Leslie declared, standing so suddenly she rocked the chair behind her.

"Wanton?" Risa frowned. "What's so wanton about looking good?"

"A man should notice a woman's inner beauty, not her outward appearance."

"Sure, but if he doesn't notice her outward appearance, he'll never get close enough to see that inward beauty."

Leslie was striding purposefully for the door. She seemed genuinely insulted, and Risa couldn't figure out why. She had only been trying to help.

"You need to read about the *strange woman* in the book of Proverbs," Leslie said, finding her coat in the closet. A moment later, she was gone with a decisive slam of the door.

Risa looked at Jodi, who now stood in the middle of the living room with her finger in her mouth. She glanced at the closed door and then at Risa.

"Where lady go?"

"Who knows," Risa sighed, then forced herself to smile

down at the little girl whose huge brown eyes regarded her with concern. "But you and I are going to the museum, so I'd better get dressed."

"Yup, we go to da musm," Jodi said, and it seemed her troubled thoughts took flight. She climbed back up onto the couch. "You get dressed," she ordered, pulling her blanket onto her lap and sucking her thumb while watching TV.

Convinced the two year old was sufficiently distracted for the next few minutes, Risa hurried to the bathroom and turned on the shower. In all honesty, she was looking forward to a few hours of touring the public museum, yet she dreaded the outing all the same. If she was really going to step aside and give Leslie a chance to capture Mike's devotion, it meant telling him good-bye this afternoon.

❧

As it happened, Mike brought Mary Beth and Tracy with him, and Risa's first thought was a negative one: *more kids, more responsibility*. However, she was pleasantly proved wrong when the teens took turns pushing Jodi in her stroller. They walked back in time through the Streets of Old Milwaukee and looked at the dinosaur exhibit. Jodi was in her glory, and Risa didn't think she'd ever seen the little girl so happy.

Around five o'clock, the small entourage made its way to the parking lot. Murmurs of starvation filled the minivan that Mike had borrowed from a friend for the day's excursion.

"How 'bout some pizza?" he suggested as they left their parking spot and drove along the downtown streets. "I know this great pizza joint."

Risa laughed. "And I suppose your cousin owns that one too."

Mike gave her a quick glance. "Second cousin."

She laughed again.

"I want a hamburger and some hot cocoa," Tracy said. "I'm sick of pizza."

"Sick of pizza?" Mike exclaimed, looking shocked. "Teenagers never get sick of pizza!"

"I want barbecued beef," Mary Beth said.

"And what do you want?" Mike asked, looking over at Risa once more.

She thought a moment. "Mm, not sure. Something hot and spicy sounds good, though."

"O–kay," Mike drawled. "Give me a few minutes to think of a place that serves all of the above."

"How 'bout my place?" Risa replied without really thinking the offer through first.

"Hey, you're on," Mike replied. "I'm dying for a home-cooked meal."

And I'm dying to cook one, Risa thought. But next she reminded herself that she was supposed to be severing her relationship with Mike. She'd all but promised Leslie.

"Ris," he said, pulling her from her thoughts, "you mentioned grocery shopping last night. . . ."

"Oh, right. I'll need to stop at a store."

"This'll be fun!" Mary Beth said from her seat directly behind Risa. "I need to learn how to cook. My stepmom just heats up frozen stuff."

"Well, I heard from a reliable source that Risa is something of a culinary expert."

She narrowed her gaze at him. "Who told you that?"

"A little bird."

Risa nodded knowingly. "I'll bet that bird was a wren. . .as in Wren Nickelson."

Mike chuckled. "You're right. And I'm jealous because you fed him and not me."

Pulling the minivan to a halt at a stoplight, he looked at her askance, and while Risa found his remark somewhat amusing, she couldn't help but think it contained some truth.

"We'll remedy that tonight, okay, Mike?"

"Okay."

"I'll cook you a feast."

He smiled, obviously mollified.

"Can we help?" Tracy wanted to know.

"Of course." Turning, she smiled at the girl and noticed then that Jodi had fallen asleep in her car seat. A nap at this late hour meant the baby would be up until midnight.

Righting herself, Risa gazed out the windshield and felt glad for the company she'd have. Mary Beth and Tracy could help occupy Jodi if nothing else. And Mike. . .well, she couldn't say she hadn't enjoyed his company this afternoon. She liked him, no question about it, and she felt flattered that he was so obviously enamored with her, something Risa hadn't experienced before. Sure, she'd had men tell her they loved her; however, hindsight revealed that they had wanted something in return for those words. Furthermore, none had been interested in a lifelong commitment.

Her gaze slid to the left, and she watched Mike as he pulled away from the stoplight. He was so different from any man she'd ever met, save for Wren, who was a born-again Christian too. But Wren hadn't ever said he loved her, and Mike had. "I think I've been in love with you since the first day I met you," he'd told her last week. Risa still had a hard time believing him. *What kind of guy falls in love with someone instantly?*

A sappy guy. A sentimental guy. One and the same.

Risa grinned inwardly, deciding she might just get very fond of sap and sentimentality.

But her next thought brought her up short. Staying out of Leslie's way might be a lot harder than she first imagined.

seventeen

"I'm so full, I think I'm going to explode!" Mike declared from his chair in Risa's kitchen.

Sitting across from him, she chuckled softly. Since the girls had wanted a quick cooking lesson, Risa decided to go all out and create her famous dish of linguine with spicy tomatoes and feta cheese. Mary Beth and Tracy were excited to learn a new recipe, and Mike had devoured a large portion, exclaiming over each bite.

"You're wonderful for a chef's ego," Risa told him. "No wonder your cousins like to see your face at their restaurants."

He chuckled. *"Mangia* was the first Italian word out of my mouth when I learned to talk."

"What's that mean, Pastor Mike?" Tracy asked from her seat on Risa's right.

"It means eat."

Everyone laughed—even Jodi, who had eaten her supper much earlier and now was perched on Tracy's lap.

"I like Italian food," Mary Beth said. "Sometimes I wish I was Italian."

"No, you don't," Mike told her. "You're special just the way you are because that's how God made you."

The girl shrugged. "I guess."

The phone rang, and Risa excused herself to answer it. Checking the Caller ID, she saw that it was her grandmother, and she winced. She hadn't talked to Nana in weeks, and she was probably in for a good tongue-lashing for her neglect. "Here's a time when I wish I wasn't Italian," she muttered before pushing the TALK button. "Ciao, Nana. What's up?"

Risa saw Mike's shoulders shake with laughter as her

grandmother's voice filled the earpiece.

"What's up? I tell you what's up. I've beena worried about you. I no hear from you for two weeks."

"I know, and I'm sorry," Risa said earnestly. "I've been busy. I'm watching Kari's little girl."

"Yah, yah, Annamarie told me."

"And I started my new job." She looked across the room at her guests. "Nana, can I call you back later? I'm kind of busy, but I promise to call."

"Yah, okay. What, you gotta man there?"

Risa grinned. "As a matter of fact, yes, I do."

A pause.

"Iz he Italian?"

"As a matter of fact, yes, he is."

Mike swiveled in his chair. Being the only "he" in the apartment, he would, of course, have figured out that Risa referred to him.

"What's hisa name?" Nana wanted to know.

"Mike Gerardi." Risa laughed at the smirk on his face. "And get this, Nana, he's a pastor. And I guess you could say we met in Italy. . . ."

Another pause.

"So, what's an Italian pastor doing ata your house? Someone dying?"

"No, Nana," she said with a laugh, "we're having dinner."

Another pause, and Risa was hard pressed to contain her mirth.

Mike shook his head at her. "Teasing your grandmother," he quietly scolded. "You should be ashamed."

Risa pointed to herself and mouthed, "Me?"

Mike nodded, but there was a glint of mischief in his dark eyes.

"So when do I meet this Italian pastor of yours?"

Covering the mouthpiece of the phone, Risa spoke to Mike. "Now you're in trouble; she wants to meet you."

"She'll adore me."

Risa made a funny face at the wisecrack, causing Mary Beth and Tracy to start giggling.

"Tell her to come and hear me preach tomorrow morning," Mike said.

"No way! She'll bring half my relations with her."

"That's okay. We'll all go out to lunch afterward."

She laughed. "How can you think of food when you've just gorged yourself?"

"Tomorrow's another day."

Her grandmother's voice heralded from the portable phone, so Risa returned it to her ear. "I'm here, Nana. And, um, you'll meet Mike. . .sometime."

"Invite her to church," he insisted.

Risa shook her head. But then at the teens' prompting, she relented. . .a little. "Mike says you should come to his church and hear him preach tomorrow morning. But you don't want to do that. It's cold outside, and you'll have to find someone to drive you. . . ."

Mike gave her a disappointed shake of his head, and the girls audibly moaned.

"Hush, over there. . . . What did you say, Nana?"

"Wheresa his church?"

"In Whitefish Bay."

"That's not far. What time?"

"Ten-fifteen." Risa looked at Mike, who nodded out the affirmative.

"Okay, lemme tell Vito, and I see you tomorrow."

"All right," Risa hedged. "But if you can't come, I will understand."

"Oh, I can come." It sounded like a threat.

Risa swallowed. "Okay, Nana, *ciao*." After sending a few kisses through the phone line, she pressed the OFF button. Looking over at Mike, she suddenly felt like the world was spinning out of control.

"Come over here and sit down," he said, waving her back to the table. "And get that horrified look off your face. Don't you think God knows what He's doing?"

Risa reclaimed her chair, feeling uncertain about how to reply. Was God in this situation? How?

"This is exciting, Miss Vitalis," Tracy said. "Is your grandmother a Christian?"

Risa nodded. "I think so."

Mike put his hand over her wrist. His touch felt warm and assuring. "Is she born again, Risa?"

She mulled over the question. "If I had to guess, I'd say no. She's not very religious."

"Well, in many ways, that's a good thing. She may be open to Bible Christianity."

"What's the difference between religion and Bible Christianity?"

"Religious practices often are simply man's way of getting to God," Mike explained. "But they don't work. The only way to the Father is through the Son, Jesus Christ."

Risa felt overwhelmed and more than a tad discouraged. She looked over at Mike. "I have so much to learn."

"And you'll learn it," he replied confidently.

But learn enough to become a pastor's wife?

As if she'd spoken the question aloud, Mike said, "Risa, it takes a lifetime to know the Bible, but you'll understand basic biblical principles soon enough." He snapped his fingers. "Which reminds me. Patti offered to watch Jodi during the week while you're at work. She also said the two of you could attend the ladies' Tuesday night Bible study at church together. David usually watches the kids while Patti's gone, and if you want to go, he doesn't mind having one more running around."

Risa gave it some thought, realizing it would be much more convenient to drive to Patti's house than to Therese's place. It would actually save her an hour's drive time there and back.

However, she knew full well that accepting Patti's kind offer meant she'd see Mike on a daily basis. She knew him well enough to guess he'd show up for dinner, and then his sister would talk Risa into staying too.

But I'm supposed to be staying out of Leslie's way. Or God's way.

Risa's head spun with confusion. What was God's way, anyhow?

Knowing Mike was waiting for an answer, she smiled. "Let me think about it, okay?"

"Sure."

Mary Beth and Tracy stood and began clearing away the dishes. They sweetly scolded Risa when she tried to help.

"I'm cleaning up," Tracy said.

"And I'm reading Jodi a story and then putting her to bed." She grinned at Mike, then at Risa. "That way you two can have some time alone together."

Both teenagers giggled.

Risa shook her head at them.

Mike stood. "How 'bout a walk, Ris?"

"Yeah, Pastor Mike needs to work off some of his linguine."

Again the giggling, but this time even Risa laughed.

"Hey, what happened to respecting your elders?" Mike shot back at the girls as he walked to the closet. Pulling out his coat, he then found Risa's and handed it to her.

With his polite assistance, she pulled it on while Mary Beth and Tracy whispered together in the kitchen. Minutes later, they made half-hearted apologies.

"Yeah, yeah. . ." Mike swept his gaze upward. Then he took hold of Risa's elbow and propelled her toward the door. "I've got my cell phone," he informed the girls. "Call if you need to, but only if you *need* to—as in life-threatening emergency. Understand?"

They nodded, and Mike closed the apartment door. He turned a triumphant smile on Risa. "Alone at last."

She smirked. "Just remember what you're preaching on tomorrow, Pastor."

"I remember, and I'll mind my manners," he replied, giving her a humble bow.

She grinned before striding to the elevator, Mike beside her. Once outside, she noticed the brisk night air, but it was mild for January.

They began walking east, toward the lakefront, and Risa silently mused about how she could break things off with Mike. Somehow, she had to make him see the futility of their relationship.

Except she suddenly realized she didn't want to break things off. Mike's friendship meant a lot to her. In a way, he replaced the friend she'd had in Kari.

On the other hand, she didn't love him. Was she leading him on or, worse, leading him down a path of destruction, as Leslie had accused?

"Mike, how does a person know if she's in God's way?"

"What?" Her inquiry had obviously caught him off guard. "In God's way?"

"Yeah, you know. . .God has this certain plan and then someone steps in and messes it up."

"Hmm. . .that's a good question. And I guess that's what prayer is all about."

"I'm not sure I even know the right way to pray," she admitted softly.

"It's easy, Risa." His voice sounded kind and gentle, warming her heart all the more. "You just talk to Jesus like you would talk to a good friend. Then you read your Bible, and that's how He talks to you."

Made sense.

They walked on through the crisp winter night. Risa snuggled deeper into her brown, gold-trimmed down jacket. "I haven't prayed at all about. . .about us."

"Well, that's okay. You've been busy. You can start

tonight. . .or even right now."

She thought about it.

"So how did this getting in God's way business come about?"

"Well, I wondered if God had a specific plan for you and maybe I was getting in the way of it. I mean, maybe God wants you to marry someone else. Someone with more experience at being a Christian."

"Maybe He does and maybe He doesn't. That's what we're supposed to be praying about, remember?"

She smiled. "I remember. I just wasn't sure how to go about it."

"For myself," Mike said, "I'm asking God to guard my steps so that when I move forward, He'll either spur me on or block my path. So far, it seems He's spurring me on. Like Friday night, for example. . like today. I really believe, Risa, that if God didn't want me to see you, He would bring about the circumstances to keep me away. . .because I'm asking Him to. . .and trusting Him to do it."

Amazingly, she felt like her load had been lifted. "So I don't have to *do* anything. I just let God do it. And the way that I would get in His way would be to go after something. . .or someone. . .and ignore the circumstances blocking my way." She thought it over. "I've been right all along."

She didn't have to look at him to see Mike's quizzical stare; she felt it. He obviously didn't quite understand her latest revelation, and perhaps she hadn't communicated it well. But it didn't matter. She understood. Perfectly. From the beginning, she hadn't wanted to be the initiator of this relationship and, therefore, she wasn't at all in God's way; however, she would be on the lookout for any speed bumps or roadblocks. And if Leslie Owens proved to be one or the other, then Risa would step aside.

Then, and only then.

The next morning, as Risa listened to Mike preach on

resisting temptation, she marveled at the way he'd interwoven the truth about their kiss into his message. It was so subtle, she didn't feel the slightest twinge of embarrassment, and if no one knew what really happened, they'd never figure it out. However, Leslie was sure to be appeased by what she heard this morning. At least Risa hoped so.

No, she *prayed* so.

Glancing down the pew, she could see that Uncle Vito was growing bored and restless, but Nana and Sharon seemed attentive. And on the other side of her grandmother sat Risa's mother and stepfather.

What a horror it had been, seeing that man again. Risa loathed and despised him, and she was still waiting for God to send a bolt from out of the blue and strike him dead. But as of yet no such miracle had occurred.

Bill Walker.

The very name made Risa feel sick. He had a lot of nerve, showing up at church—especially this church. Nana wouldn't have invited him. She knew better. Even Risa's mother knew better. So why had he come?

Turning her attention back to Mike, Risa fought to gain control of her emotions and pay attention. She'd been successful thus far; however, after the service, there were sure to be fireworks.

Mike wrapped up his message and everyone bowed their heads while a gentleman in the congregation prayed. It was quite a lengthy monologue, and when the "Amen!" finally sounded, Risa looked up and found Mike standing beside her.

"Good message, Pastor Gerardi," she said with mock formality. But it seemed to fit, since Mike was attired in a charcoal gray suit, crisp white dress shirt, and coordinating red and black tie. "You did a fine job."

He seemed pleased to hear it. "Really think so?"

Risa nodded.

"Praise the Lord!"

"But now you'll have to excuse me," she said, feeling her smile slip away. "I'm about to verbally rip my stepfather to shreds."

Mike's cocoa brown gaze grew wide. "Whoa! No ripping allowed."

Risa shook her head. "This isn't funny, Mike. I'm serious."

"So am I." His voice became a whisper. "Look, you told me something about him, and—"

"And that wasn't even the half of it." Risa fought against the tears threatening to escape her eyes.

"Okay, I believe you. But there are better ways to handle this situation than to lose your temper."

"Lose? It's *lost!*"

"Risa, calm down."

She bristled at the warning. Then, from behind her, she heard Sharon politely clear her throat.

"Are you going to introduce us?"

Risa turned to see a line of her relatives waiting to get out of the pew and into the aisle. "Oh, yes. . .sorry."

Tamping down her anger, which was no small feat, she introduced Mike to her family. She even presented her mother, but when it came to Bill, she simply pretended he wasn't there. Mike, however, was quick to pick up the ball where she'd purposely let it drop.

Watching the two men shake hands, Risa felt deeply betrayed. If Mike really loved her, he'd take her side. He would understand her pain and all she'd suffered. Her stepfather had been an abusive alcoholic, and if Mike couldn't comprehend the emotional scarring Risa carried to this day, he could at least try to be sympathetic.

She turned on her heel and left the sanctuary, heading for the nursery to fetch Jodi. She felt overwhelmed with sadness.

There's my roadblock, she thought.

eighteen

"Hey, I thought we were going out for lunch," Mike said as he strode toward Risa in the church parking lot. January snow crunched under the weight of his every step. He reached the car. "Risa?"

She ignored him, and Mike knew she was angry. Oh, he'd known she was upset about her stepfather showing up for the service—that obviously *had* been quite a surprise. But Mike never dreamed she'd be mad at him. He hadn't done anything wrong!

"Ris, what's up?"

She finished buckling Jodi into the car seat, straightened, and turned to face him. To his amazement she didn't appear angry. She looked hurt, sad, and vulnerable.

"You know what we talked about last night? About God putting circumstances in our way?"

Mike felt his gut tighten. "Yeah. What about it?"

"I think this is that circumstance, Mike. That roadblock showing us this relationship isn't meant to be."

"Why's that?" he asked softly.

She gazed off somewhere over his left shoulder, and Mike got the distinct impression that she was doing her best to hold back the tears.

"I've got issues."

"Okay," he said, "let's deal with them one by one."

Risa shook her head. "You don't understand."

"Enlighten me."

Her hazel eyes darkened, and now Mike thought she *did* seem angry.

"You shook his hand, Mike—like he was your friend."

"I was trying to be polite."

"Why? I told you about him. Why would you want to be polite to that. . .that jerk?"

"You need to forgive your stepfather, Risa." The words were out before Mike even thought about them. And they obviously were not what she wanted to hear.

"Never. Do you hear me? I will never forgive him for what he did to me." Her voice was barely above a whisper. "He'd get drunk and slap me around the living room, call me names, pull my hair. I couldn't go to school for three days one time because he gave me a black eye."

Mike grimaced and rubbed a hand over his jaw. "Oh, man, Risa, I'm sorry." He drew in a deep breath. "But you know what? You still have to forgive him. . .just like God, for Christ's sake, forgave you for every sin you ever committed."

"See? That's what I mean," she replied, piercing him with an icy glare. "You and I are miles apart, Mike, and as far as I can see, there's no spanning the gap."

Spinning on her heel, she walked around the car, opened the door, and climbed in behind the wheel.

Mike felt as helpless as Jodi was—strapped securely in her car seat, unable to control anything in her environment—and his heart filled with sorrow as he watched Risa drive away.

Glancing around the emptying lot, he made his way back into the church. Maybe it really *was* over between him and Risa; but maybe it wasn't. He thought maybe he should let her cool down and then try to talk to her again; or maybe he should leave her alone. Mike knew his feelings for her outweighed hers for him, but that didn't stop him from hoping and praying.

He reached the foyer where Risa's grandmother, aunt, and uncle stood, chatting with Patti and David. Her mother and stepfather had already left. Seeing Mike approach, the remaining five turned expectant gazes on him.

"Well, she's upset," Mike announced. "She went home."

"Yah, I knew it," the old woman said.

"I'm just surprised Risa didn't make a scene," Sharon added with a wry smile. "I really thought we were going to see some drama there at the end of the church service."

Mike couldn't help but grin.

"Really not like Risa at all," her uncle stated, wearing a puzzled frown. "She lets her temper flare and doesn't care who's around when she does it."

Her family can see a change in her, Mike realized. And that was all the little bit of hope he needed. He wasn't ready to give up quite yet.

Smiling at Risa's gray-haired grandmother, he said, "May I take you to lunch? All of you? My treat. I know this great little place downtown—best eggplant Parmesan you ever tasted."

The old woman grinned and looked at her son. "Know what? I lika this man!"

&

By six o'clock that evening, Risa was seething. She phoned Arlene and didn't ask but *told* her she would have to watch Jodi for awhile.

"I've got something I need to take care of."

Arlene had the good sense not to balk.

Upon arrival at the woman's house, Risa had a talk with Jodi and sensed that somehow the little girl understood. Risa had made up her mind to confront her stepfather, and Jodi would just have to stay with her grandmother for the next couple of hours.

"And you'll be back to pick her up?" Arlene asked as she stood by the front door, clad in a pair of navy stirrup pants and an oversized, multicolored sweater.

"I'll be back." Risa tried to ignore Jodi's mournful brown eyes that were beginning to fill with tears.

"She'll be all right," Arlene assured Risa. Then she grinned. "Just make it fast."

Feeling more aggravated than ever, Risa drove to her

mother and stepfather's house, a single-story ranch on the northwest side of Milwaukee. She rang the doorbell and shoved her hands into her jacket pockets as she waited for someone to answer.

She glanced around the tiny porch and the snow-covered lawn and realized she hated this house. Always had. But it wasn't the house's fault. Rather, the blame lay on the man who owned it.

Growing impatient, Risa pressed on the bell again and, moments later, the front door opened, revealing her mother in a pink, woolly robe.

"Risa, what are you doing here?" She opened the door wider.

"I want to talk to Bill."

"Well, um. . ." She appeared skeptical and glanced over her shoulder. Finally, she shrugged. "Sure. Come on in."

Risa stepped across the threshold and wiped her feet on the mat in the front hallway.

"I hope you're not here to start the third world war."

"You know me so well, don't you?"

Her mother inhaled sharply at the barbed reply, and Risa felt guilty immediately. Clare hadn't been the best mom, but the woman standing before her with fashionably cropped black hair was still her mother.

"Sorry. I shouldn't have spoken to you like that."

"Apology accepted." Taking a step backward, Clare called for her husband. "We've got company." She turned a smile on Risa. "Have a seat."

"No, thanks. This won't take long."

"Oh, dear," her mother murmured.

Minutes went by, and at last Bill Walker stepped into the living room. He was a tall, slim man, except for his round belly, which protruded from beneath his flannel shirt and over his tan trousers. His dark eyes were set a bit too far apart on his wide face, and he had always reminded Risa of a reptile.

"Well, Risa," Bill said, "what a surprise."

She narrowed her gaze. She hadn't seen her stepfather in years, and somehow he didn't seem like much of a threat as he fairly shuffled over to the sofa and sat down. His breath came quickly, as if the simple act had winded him.

"Bill's been sick," Clare explained as if divining her daughter's thoughts.

"So sorry to hear that," Risa said, each word laced with sarcasm.

"He's got pancreatic cancer. There's nothing the doctors can do, and he's been in awful pain."

Risa looked at her mother. "I hope you don't expect any sympathy from me."

"Oh, Risa," Clare said, tears filling her eyes. "Why did you come here?"

"Why did you and Bill come to church this morning?" she countered. "Who invited you?"

"No one," Bill said from his perch on the couch. "Sharon talked to your mother last night, and when we found out you were dating a pastor, I started hoping. . ."

"Hoping what?"

"Hoping that. . ." Bill raked a hand over his bald head, and Risa noticed the yellow hue of his complexion. "I started hoping you'd forgive me for all the. . .the terrible things I did," he managed.

Risa grunted out a laugh. "The day pigs fly, that'll be the day I forgive you. And I only came here to tell you to stay out of my life. Forever!"

"I think it's time for you to leave," Clare said, moving toward the door.

Risa turned to go.

"No, wait!" Bill rose from the couch. "Wait, Risa. Just hear me out, and then I promise I'll never bother you again. Just listen. Please."

"Listen to what?"

"I faced my demons," he said. "I was a lousy drunk. I hurt

your mother and you, and I'm paying for it with my health. My liver is shot and it won't be long, the doctors say, before I die when my pancreas fails. Could be days. Maybe a few weeks."

"Spare me the sob story." She took a step toward the door.

"Wait, Risa."

She paused.

"About five years ago, I went through a program for alcoholics. Your mother went with me. It was free through the church down the street. We received some good counseling, and in the process, we became Christians."

Slowly, Risa turned to face her stepfather. "You're born again?"

He smiled and nodded. "Your mother too."

Risa glanced at Clare, who wiped an errant tear from her cheek. "That's right, Honey."

Looking back at Bill Walker, all Risa could think about was how unfair it seemed that now she would have to share heaven with such a scum like him.

"Risa, God forgave me," her stepfather said. "Now, I'm asking you to do the same. Can you? Will you?"

"No," she replied.

With that, she left the house, wishing she'd never gone there in the first place.

nineteen

Dark January days crept slowly by, and Risa began to feel blue. She left for work each morning before the sun was up and came home long after it had set. Jodi, on the other hand, didn't seem to mind her new schedule at Therese's house, even though she occasionally asked that heartrending question, "Where Mommy go?"

There were times when Risa felt so tired and frustrated that she wanted to call Arlene or Kari's sister, or even José, Jodi's father, and tell them *they* could watch the little stinker for awhile. Legally, of course, Jodi was their responsibility. But each time she felt the notion coming on, she squelched it, fearing the two year old wouldn't receive the proper care.

So she pressed on, but wondered how long she could continue this stressful arrangement.

One Thursday evening, she talked Therese into keeping Jodi overnight so that she could go out right after work and meet some girlfriends for dinner. She hadn't seen these gals since she'd quit at the USPS. But oddly, Risa didn't enjoy herself, and that, compounded by the fact that she refused to drink anything but cola, caused her friends to question her.

"Look, guys, I've just decided to stay away from alcoholic beverages. It's just something. . .something I feel I need to do."

They knew a bit about her past, so Risa told them about what happened in Italy, Kari's death, how she'd met Mike there, and how they'd dated afterward.

"But it didn't work out," she concluded.

"Probably for the best," Shelley said, sipping her margarita. Her long blond hair was in a fat braid that fell down the length of her slender back, and she still wore her post office garb. "And it's a good thing you found out after only a few dates."

"Yeah," Risa replied. However, her heart didn't seem to agree. She wished Mike would call her, but she hadn't heard from him in weeks now. She thought about calling him, but worried about getting in somebody's way.

"You know what I'd do?" ebony-haired Judy began as she waved a long red fingernail at her. "I'd tell Kari's family to pick up that kid and quit acting so irresponsible."

"I've had the same idea," Risa agreed, "but what about Jodi?"

"Oh, kids are adaptable little things," Dawn said after a swallow of beer. She tucked a portion of her strawberry blond hair behind her ear and her blue eyes twinkled. "My four kids have adjusted fine to spending one weekend with their dad and the next with me. They're even starting to get along with Tim," she added, referring to her live-in boyfriend.

Risa forced a smile at each of her friends, knowing they were trying to cheer her up; however, she'd never felt more discouraged in her life. She knew what it was like to be ping-ponged back and forth between parents, and while she might have seemed "adjusted" to the adults around her, she knew now that her emotions had been a mess all through her growing-up years—especially since she'd been forced to put up with Bill Walker.

Could Risa really do that to Jodi? But what was the alternative?

As for Mike, her heart sank deeper into despair when she thought that maybe she'd blown her one and only chance to find a decent guy who really loved her.

But of course, if it wasn't meant to be. . .

"Have a drink," Judy said. "It'll make you feel better."

Risa shook her head. "Alcohol won't solve my problems," she murmured, staring into her cola. "Only God can fix my situation."

When she didn't hear any of the ladies around her respond, she glanced up. To Risa's surprise, each of her friends wore an incredulous expression.

"What's wrong?" she asked.

"*God's* going to fix your situation?" Judy repeated. She laughed. "Girl, you might as well get yourself a magic wand."

They all found the remark amusing—all but Risa. And suddenly her close friends didn't seem so close anymore. They didn't understand her. However, Mike would. So would Patti and David. So would those two adorable teens, Mary Beth and Tracy.

She sat at the table with the ladies awhile longer. Then, at an opportune moment, Risa glanced at her watch. "Oh, gotta go." She really wasn't pressed for time, but she couldn't sit here in this dimly lit barroom another minute. "Nice seein' you guys again."

They shared good-byes and made Risa promise to keep in touch.

Slinging her purse strap over her shoulder, she grabbed her coat and left. Outside, she breathed in the frozen air, glad to be out of the smoky environment. And in that moment, Risa found herself at a place of decision. She could go back into the bar and pretend the past three months had never happened, or she could walk away, knowing she was a changed woman because she'd given her soul to God.

Well, I'm certainly not taking it back, she thought. And what had her former lifestyle ever done for her anyway? She'd lived through one heartbreak after another.

She walked to her car, parked a block away. *Lord Jesus, I don't know if I'm praying the right way, but it's the best I can do. Mike said You're my friend. . .and I believe it's true because I sure can't relate to my old friends anymore.* She climbed into her car and started the engine. *I need You, Lord Jesus, because at this moment I feel so totally, utterly alone. . .and I need a friend.*

When she arrived at her apartment, the time was fast approaching eight o'clock. Risa felt grateful for the evening of quiet she'd have ahead, since Jodi was with Therese and her brood.

Kicking off her heels, Risa padded to the couch and turned on the television. The first picture that flashed across the screen was a bed scene, courtesy of one of the weekly dramas.

"Oh, lovely," she muttered, flipping off the set with the remote control. "A person can't even watch TV these days."

Collapsing against the leather sofa, her gaze suddenly fell on her rainbow Bible, sitting on the shelf across the room where a certain two year old couldn't reach it. She decided that maybe she should spend the night reading God's promises. After all, His Word had made her feel better when she'd previously read it.

She fetched the book from its perch, remembering that the last time she'd opened it had been the Sunday Mike preached. . . and her jerk of a stepfather had shown up. Opening the Bible to Genesis, she commenced reading where she'd left off.

Moments later, she had a thought: Maybe she ought to go to that Tuesday night Bible study Mike had said Patti attended. That would be a night out, and Risa figured she needed the break. Moreover, she'd be among friends. New friends.

But what about Mike?

After several thoughtful moments, Risa chided herself. The man was unavoidable. Hadn't he proven that already? She might as well face any looming consequences head-on. If she ran into him in the church hallway as she walked to the Bible study, then so be it. If he happened to be with Leslie, she'd just have to deal with that.

Walking to her desk, Risa found the telephone book and flipped through its pages until she found Patti Kreske's number. She hoped it wasn't too late to call.

"Risa! How nice to hear from you again," Patti said upon

answering the phone and learning the caller was Risa.

"Hey, same here."

"What are you up to these days?"

"Pretty much the same old thing. Say, I'm interested in that Tuesday night Bible study you mentioned one time."

"Great. We'd love for you to come! Let me give you the particulars."

Risa wrote down the details.

"Oh, and I've got to tell you this. . .you know Leslie Owens?"

"Yes?" Risa's stomach suddenly felt like it had been tied in knots.

"Well, she got this new hairdo a few weeks ago. . ."

Took my suggestion, eh? Risa thought, unable to help a small grin.

". . .and she looks like a million bucks. We had a guest speaker last Sunday—he's a single missionary, working in South Africa. I think he's the tallest guy I've ever seen! And would you believe he fell head over heels in love with Leslie? I mean, talk about love at first sight!"

"No kidding?" Risa sighed, willing her heart to slow its rapid beats.

"So they are now officially 'courting,' and Mike told me this fella is going to be hanging around awhile. . .on furlough." Patti chuckled.

"That's great. . . . So, um, how's Mike doing, anyway?" Risa had to ask.

"Keeping busy. You know him. He's always up to something. Tonight, it's men's basketball."

"Well, I miss him," Risa admitted.

"Yeah?" Patti paused. "Well, he misses you too. I've been telling him to call you, but he keeps saying he doesn't want to push. And, Risa, I think Mike wants Jesus to be your first love."

Tears gathered in Risa's eyes. "Jesus is my first love. I mean,

He's got my soul."

"And no man can pluck it out of His hand."

"That's very comforting." Risa smiled, wiping a tear from her cheek. "So, what time does the men's basketball game end?"

Patti laughed, as if she understood the plot floating around Risa's brain. "Pretty soon. David is usually home by ten o'clock."

"Hmm. . ."

"Thinking of stopping by?"

"Think I should?"

"Most definitely."

Risa grinned. "Okay, I'm off. And. . .thanks, Patti."

❧

The sound of a bouncing basketball led Risa to the gym inside Bay Community Church. She'd been there before, although her memory wasn't clear as to its exact location, so she was glad for the deep male grunts of effort, the loud cheers or groans following a shot, and the squeak of athletic shoes on the polished wood floor that provided extra direction.

Shrugging out of her heavy overcoat, she stood at the doorway, observing the players. She picked out Mike's dark head right away. From this distance she could see that his baby blue T-shirt was sweat stained and his gray, baggy sweatpants were in similar condition. She suddenly had a feeling he might not like her dropping in on him when he didn't look his best. However, she quickly decided Mike wasn't that vain.

In the next moment he saw her, and his dark gaze locked with hers. He stopped in midmotion, then turned and muttered an explanation to one of his buddies before grabbing a towel off the floor at the sidelines and heading her way.

Risa didn't think he looked pleased to see her. Perhaps her initial instinct had been accurate after all.

"Risa! What are you doing here?" Mike said, sounding winded.

"Patti said I'd find you here."

"Wren's here," Mike interjected.

"Oh, yeah?" Risa suddenly knew the reason for Mike's displeasure. "I had no idea."

"Nancie had an appointment somewhere nearby, so Wren thought he'd join us."

"How nice." Risa felt a bit awkward, knowing Wren was but several yards away; however, awkward is all she felt. "I didn't come to see Wren," she stated in all honesty. "I came to see you."

She could see in Mike's eyes that he didn't believe her.

"I had no idea that Wren would be here."

Mike didn't reply, just continued to gaze at her with the same look of disbelief.

She shook her head, feeling like dissolving into tears out of sheer disappointment. "Oh, forget it. I shouldn't have come."

She whirled around and walked back down the corridor. But then she couldn't resist launching a two-pointer of her own. "Tell Wren hello from me," she tossed over her shoulder in the most seductive voice she could muster.

With that she left the building, telling herself she didn't care if the shot had made its mark. Guys could be such jerks. . .even pastors.

As she reached the car, it occurred to Risa that women could be jerks too. *I'm sorry, Lord. I guess I hit another roadblock.*

❧

"Wren, just knock me out and put me out of my misery. I'm a jealous fool; what can I say?"

He grinned. "You might start with 'I'm sorry.' I've found that those words do wonders."

Mike sighed. "She said she came to see me. That's what I've been waiting for. But all I could think of was that she had somehow found out you were here, and—"

"And that's impossible, because this was a spur-of-the-moment thing." Wren took a gulp from his sports drink, then wiped his mouth on the towel hanging around his neck. "No one knew I was coming. . .not even me, until the last minute, when I pulled into the church parking lot. I'm just glad I had my gym stuff in the trunk."

Sitting on the bleachers beside his friend, Mike put his head in his hands and rubbed his tired eyes. "Risa's ticked off at me. No doubt about it. And I deserve it." He recalled the barb she'd thrown at him as she walked away. If he hadn't been jealous-mad before, he'd felt downright incensed then— and that had been her intention. Dressed in a black knit skirt and matching sweater, she had made a fetching sight, one Mike didn't want to share with any other guy.

However, it didn't take him long to realize his mistake.

"Man, I can't believe it."

"Hey, look," Wren said, combing fingers through his nut brown hair. "If you're serious about Risa, which I can tell you are, then you'd better just accept the fact that this isn't the last time the two of you are going to irritate each other. Learn to apologize for your part and forgive her for hers, and be done with it."

Mike grinned. "You speak from experience, eh?"

"You'd better believe it. But from what I recall, Risa is very forgiving."

"On the contrary. She refuses to forgive her stepfather. I'm probably next on her blacklist."

Wren winced. "I forgot about her stepdad. She really hates that guy."

"Yep."

In the next moment, Wren's face split into a grin. "But she really trusted Christ, huh?"

Mike nodded.

"That's so cool. Wait until I tell Nancie. We've both been praying for Risa's salvation."

"Like any new babe in Christ, she's got a ways to go."

Wren shrugged. "Yeah, but so did Nancie, and now she's

more spiritual than I am. Now *she* quotes Scripture to *me* whenever trials arise, and the girls think it's a hoot."

A slow smile spread across Mike's face. "How's your latest addition?"

"Sarah Joy? Great. She's getting big. Alexa and Laura think she's the best baby doll they ever had to play with. Sometimes I wince when I see Laura carrying her around. I think she's going to drop her. But at the same time, it's really cute. Laura acts just like a little mother."

Mike nodded, still smiling.

"Okay, so are you going to call Risa or what?"

"Wanna call her for me?" Mike teased.

Wren laughed. "Not particularly. I've got my own set of females to deal with."

"Guess you're right."

Wren gave him a friendly clap between the shoulder blades. "Buck up. You can do it."

Mike sucked in an apprehensive breath. Risa would have every good reason to tell him to take a long walk off a short pier—and she wasn't too shy to say something like that, either.

"Maybe I'll let her cool down for awhile."

"Come on, you chicken," Wren prompted. "I've got a few minutes before I have to pick up Nancie and the girls. Let's go into your office and make the phone call."

"Moral support. . .yeah, that's what I need."

"You need more like a dozen roses, Buster, but let's give the phone call a try anyway."

Deciding Wren was right, Mike laughed, stood, and then exited the gym with his friend walking beside him.

twenty

Risa ignored Mike's phone calls for the next few days. She knew she was being stubborn, but she couldn't seem to get past the memory of those pools of doubt that had filled Mike's eyes that night at the gym. Did he really think she'd seek Wren out, knowing he was married? Did he really believe she'd stoop that low?

She had felt betrayed before, when Mike welcomed her stepfather at church so heartily, but this went beyond the pain of insult to the point where Risa actually felt wounded.

"I think you shoulda marry him," Nana said that Saturday afternoon as they took care of last-minute wedding preparations for Annamarie. The topic of weddings prompted Nana to think of a match for Risa. . .namely, Mike. "He's a nice-a young man."

"A pastor, Risa?" Her cousin was all smiles and wide-eyed interest.

"Yeah, a pastor, and he's nice, all right. But I don't think there's any hope for us. I mean, he's got two major strikes against him right now. Three strikes and he's out."

Annamarie laughed. "Let's hear it for unconditional love! Yea!"

"What do you mean?" she asked with a frown.

"She means you oughta forgiva him."

That word again, she thought. *Forgiveness.*

Last night, she'd read the end of the book of Genesis, the story of Joseph. He had forgiven his brothers for selling him into slavery. Had it been her, Risa would have wanted them to be publicly flogged—or whatever punishment was equivalent to that at the time. But Joseph welcomed them back, saying,

"You intended to harm me, but God intended it for good."

And then this morning, Risa had flipped over the little daily calendar she had purchased at the store when she bought her Bible. Today's verse was, "And be ye kind one to another, tenderhearted, forgiving one another, even as God for Christ's sake hath forgiven you." Risa recalled Mike saying something like that to her in the parking lot when she was fuming over strike number one.

"So, Risa," Annamarie said, wearing a little smirk. "Tell me about this guy."

"Nothing to tell," she replied tersely. "Let's get on with your wedding plans. Do we have all the gifts for the attendants?"

"I'lla tell you about him," Nana said.

And for the next half-hour, Risa was forced to listen to Mike Gerardi's glowing attributes. It wasn't until suppertime that they got around to discussing Annamarie's wedding, which would soon be upon them.

When Risa arrived home that night, the phone was ringing. Carrying a sleeping Jodi in her arms, along with a diaper bag and purse, she didn't rush to answer it, but set down her bags and carefully lay Jodi on the sofa, where she slipped off her snowsuit. The caller didn't leave a message, and Risa assumed it was Mike. Then, minutes later, the phone rang again.

With Jodi tucked into bed, Risa checked the Caller ID. Seeing that it was her mother, curiosity got the better of her, and she pressed the TALK button.

"Oh, Risa, I'm so glad you're home. Bill's in the hospital. He's probably not going to make it through the night."

Risa fought against a caustic reply.

"This is your last chance," her mother said in a strained voice. "If you come now, you might still be able to talk to him. . .to forgive him. He's in and out of consciousness. Oh, Risa," her mother said, breaking down and weeping, "your bitterness will only end up eating you alive. Don't you see that?"

Tears filled her eyes, but every fiber of Risa's being screamed, *No!* She didn't want to forgive the man she'd hated for more than half her life. Yet that subtle inner prompting, that little inward nudge, told her she had to go.

"I have to get someone to watch Jodi."

Her mother sniffed. "Okay. Just hurry, Risa. Please?"

Clicking off the phone, Risa had to think fast.

Patti.

Finding the Kreskes' number, she punched it into the phone. Patti answered, and after hearing Risa's predicament, she suggested Mary Beth Canfield as a possible baby-sitter. Patti then gave Risa the teen's phone number.

"Thanks. I know I have her number around here somewhere. . . . Oh, and, um, do you know if Mike is at home by any chance?" Suddenly Risa wanted him there. . .no, she *needed* him to come to the hospital with her. She didn't think she could face this alone.

"I think Mike's at church," his sister replied. "He's usually there studying Saturday nights."

Risa decided to phone him there. . .right after she called Mary Beth.

As it happened, the girl was at Tracy's house, and Risa obtained that number from Mary Beth's father. When she called the Schmidts' home, she talked to John and only partially revealed the circumstances. But that was enough. He offered to drop both girls off at Risa's place, saving her the trouble of bundling up Jodi again in order to fetch them. By the time the teens arrived, Risa felt frazzled. She hadn't been able to get hold of Mike, so she'd have to stop at the church before rushing to the hospital.

"Thanks, guys," she said, grabbing her coat and purse. "Eat whatever you want."

"We'll be praying for you. . .and your stepfather," Tracy said as Risa ran out the door.

In her car, she sped to Bay Community Church, praying she wouldn't get a ticket on the way. *Lord Jesus, please help me*, she prayed. *Help me forgive Bill. . .and Mike. . .and I hope Mike can forgive me too.*

Parking her car, Risa found the side door of the church unlocked and entered the building. She stopped dead in her tracks, hearing the *bonk, bonk, bonk, swish* of someone shooting hoops in the gym. She hesitantly moved forward, unsure whom she'd find there. To her delight, relief, and mild trepidation, it was Mike. He was dressed in black casual pants and a blue dress shirt whose tails had come untucked. Standing at the doorway, Risa grinned at the sight. He looked like a boy whose mother had dressed him for Sunday school, but he'd sneaked out to play instead. Then, all too soon, she was reminded of what lay ahead of her tonight.

She cleared her throat. "Mike?"

He swung around at the sound of her voice, basketball in hand. "Risa?"

For the next moment, neither of them moved, and she realized he was waiting for her to speak first. To apologize, perhaps. But she felt so overwhelmed and, yes, even scared, that all she could do was stand there and let the tears spill from her eyes.

Looking alarmed, Mike dropped the basketball and jogged toward her. "What's wrong? What is it?"

"My stepfather's d—dying," she managed to croak out. "He's in the hospital. W—will you come with me?"

His expression softened. "Let me get my coat."

❧

An eerie silence prevailed in the hospital room as Risa stood at Bill Walker's bedside. Mike was next to her, her mother facing them on the other side of the bed.

"Bill? Risa is here," Clare said, stroking the man's forehead.

His eyelids fluttered ever so slightly.

Clare gave Risa a nod of encouragement. "Talk to him. See if he'll wake up."

She swallowed before casting an uncertain glance at Mike.

He put a reassuring hand on her shoulder. "Go ahead, Ris."

"Bill?" Risa's voice sounded shaky to her own ears. "Bill, it's Risa. I—I came to. . .well. . ."

Suddenly a conversation she'd had with Mary Beth flitted across her mind. It had taken place shortly after Kari's death. The teen described her drug-addicted stepmother, then told Risa how she'd forgiven the woman for stealing her baby-sitting money.

Forgiveness. God commanded it.

"Bill," Risa tried again, "I came here tonight to tell you that. . .that I forgive you, okay?" She spoke the words out of obedience to God, but she didn't necessarily *feel* them. "The past is dead and gone, and we can't change it. But we can change who we are and have a new life in Christ. I know that's the case with both of us. . . ." Risa thought she was beginning to ramble.

Then, as if it were taking an extraordinary amount of effort to open his eyes, Bill's lids parted halfway. A little grin curved his thin, dry lips.

At that moment, as Risa stared at him, her hate waned with each passing second. Suddenly, empathy took its place. She realized that here in this hospital bed lay a dying man, one who had suffered physically for his transgressions. Wasn't that enough punishment for him here on earth? Risa thought it was, and suddenly she felt glad that Bill's eternity wouldn't be filled with pain.

Her shaky fingertips touched her stepfather's ham-sized hand. "Everything's right between you and me now, Bill," she said with tears suddenly clouding her vision. "I forgive you—completely."

As if in direct reply, the muscles in the failing man's face relaxed. His eyes closed. He looked at peace.

He looked ready to go home.

❧

"You're a brave woman, and I'm really proud of you for what you did tonight," Mike said later.

Risa grinned. "Thanks."

"Do you know this might impact generations to come?"

Slouched in a vinyl chair in the waiting area, Risa watched

Mike purchase two cups of coffee from the vending machine. "How do you figure?"

"Well, you told me that there's a rift between the Vitalis family and the Mandelinis because of how your stepdad treated you. But now that you've forgiven him, you can share the news with your father's side of the family. Healing can begin there too. Perhaps it'll open doors for you to share Christ with that side of the family. What if they get saved, Risa, because of what happened tonight?"

"Do you really think that's possible?"

"All things are possible with God."

"I won't argue with that."

Mike smiled. Then, holding a steaming cup of coffee in each hand, he made his way to her, gave her one, and sat down.

Risa pushed herself up and turned toward him. "Mike, I'm sorry for everything. . .I mean, between you and me."

"It's me who owes *you* an apology," he replied.

"And I'm sure you would have given me one if I'd answered my phone."

"Risa, I was jealous that night at the gym, and I had no reason for it. I was wrong."

She couldn't help the hint of a grin tugging at her mouth. She felt oddly flattered by Mike's admission. She stared into her coffee before glancing over at him. "And I was wrong for making the situation worse."

After a rueful smile, he sipped his coffee. "Well, all's forgiven on this end."

"This end too."

Sitting back, Risa took a drink from the cup in her hand. "Don't be jealous of Wren. I'm not in love with him."

"That's music to my ears," Mike said, his smile broadening.

Once more, she glanced over at him, feeling grateful for his support tonight, grateful for his friendship.

"I've missed you," she said in a soft voice.

He met her gaze. "I've missed you too."

His words warmed her heart, and in that moment, she

knew she didn't want to face the rest of her life without him.

"We'd better be going," he said, looking at his watch. "Morning comes awfully fast, and tomorrow is the Lord's day."

She nodded and allowed Mike to help her to her feet. Collecting their coats, they bid Clare good night as she continued her vigil by Bill's bedside.

"I'll let you know if there's any change," she promised.

Both Risa and Mike nodded, then they left the hospital.

On the way home, Risa was silent, prayerfully silent. She knew her emotions were in high gear, and she didn't want to say anything that she'd have to take back later. Nevertheless, the words were on the tip of her tongue—*I love you.*

She loved Mike. How could she not? He was there for her night and day. If she sounded the alarm, he dropped whatever he was doing and answered the call. He was a modern-day knight in shining armor. Sure, he was a bit impetuous at times. And, yes, he liked to preach on everything that came up. But Risa was getting used to it, and she even enjoyed his sermons because she believed in God's rainbow promises now.

Besides, Nana liked him.

They reached the church, and Mike opened the passenger door. "Will I see you tomorrow?" he asked.

Risa nodded.

"Good." He climbed out of the car. "Plan to come to Patti's house afterward. My sister Roselle will be there too."

"Okay."

He began closing the door, but then opened it upon an apparent afterthought. "I should warn you, my parents will most likely be there also. But don't let that keep you away."

"I don't scare that easily, Mike," she said with a broad smile.

He chuckled. "I didn't think so. Good night."

" 'Night."

Risa watched him walk to the side entrance of the church and go inside. She sat there in the parking lot, feeling as though something important had been left undone. That little nudge. That inner prompting.

"Oh, all right," she muttered, opening her car door. "I'll go tell him."

She paused in midstride. *But do I really mean it?*

In the next moment, she tried to imagine what her future without Mike would be like. What if there was another Leslie Owens waiting in the wings? What if she snatched him away? Risa knew right then that her heart would be irreparably shattered, although she also believed Mike loved her too much to simply take flight with another woman. Her knight was as faithful as they come.

So what more could she ask for in a guy?

With renewed determination, Risa quickened her pace and entered the church. She walked through the darkened corridor, passed by the gym, then found her way into the church's office suites. The first door on her right was closed, but the next stood open, and from her vantage point, Risa could see Mike hanging up his coat.

She stepped forward and knocked on the door frame.

Mike glanced up and smiled. "Risa. What are you doing here? I thought you went home."

"I wanted to say thanks for coming to the hospital with me tonight."

"You're welcome." His gaze darkened. "You know I'd do just about anything for you."

"Yeah, I know." Risa looked at the tops of her leather ankle boots and felt herself blush, an odd sensation for her. She glanced back up at him. "You're a sweet guy, Mike, and. . .I love you. I mean that. I love you."

He looked at her so hard, Risa wondered if he'd heard her. Next, she wondered if he was going to break into tears, and she couldn't stand the thought of that happening.

She crossed the room and put her hands on his upper arms, giving him a mild shake. "Oh, now, don't get all mushy on me."

"It seems like I've waited a lifetime to hear those words." He smiled at her with bleary eyes. "I love you too, Risa."

"I know. . .and that only makes me love you all the more." She let go of his arms and placed her hands in his, intertwining their fingers.

"Will you marry me?" he asked so tenderly that Risa felt she might cry.

Not trusting her voice, she nodded.

"You will? Really?"

She laughed at his incredulous look. "What did you think I'd say, no?"

He shrugged. "I hoped it would be yes. That's why I asked. But there's always that chance."

"Not this time. You're too good a guy to let get away."

"Glad you think so."

They gazed into each other's eyes for the briefest of moments before hearing the door to the neighboring office open. They both turned to see Kevin Batzler.

"Hey, you two want to keep it down in here?" he said, looking mildly irritated. "I'm working on my sermon for tomorrow."

"Sorry, Kev. Risa just agreed to marry me. I'm rejoicing."

The other pastor smiled. "Well, congratulations. When's the wedding?"

"Soon," Mike replied.

Risa laughed at his impatience. But then she thought of Annamarie's wedding coming up in less than two weeks.

She looked up into Mike's face. "You don't think we could get married before Valentine's Day, do you?"

He shrugged, wearing a sheepish grin. "The sooner the better, as far as I'm concerned."

"Oh, no, never mind. I'm being selfish."

Mike crossed his arms, narrowing his gaze. "What's on your mind, Ris?"

"Well, I always wanted to be married before my cousin Annamarie, and her wedding is on the fourteenth, and—"

"Annamarie?" Mike frowned. "Is she the same Annamarie who's marrying Tony Bartelli?"

"Yes!" Risa gaped at him.

"Tony's my cousin," Mike said with a grin. "I'm the one who talked him into tying the knot."

"Really? Good job. Took long enough, though."

Kevin laughed and shook his head. "Good night. I'm going back to study."

"Thanks, Kev," Mike called. "We'll be quieter."

"If it gets too quiet, I'm going to worry."

Risa smiled, and Mike chuckled.

"No kidding," he said once Kevin's office door closed. "The two of us are standing up in our cousins' wedding. Small world, eh?"

"Yeah, small world." Risa smiled into Mike's eyes. "But you know what? It doesn't really matter to me when I marry you, just as long as it really happens. I want to spend the rest of my life with you."

"Even if it means being a pastor's wife?" he said, a twinkle in his dark eyes.

"Oh, that?" she said, waving the issue away. "Granted, I have a lot to learn, but you can teach me."

"And the Lord will open your understanding," Mike said, all humor aside. "Faithful is he that calleth you, who also will do it."

"I'm *called* to be a pastor's wife?" A shock went through Risa, and she experienced a moment of awe. A pastor's wife? She would never have thought it in her wildest of dreams, yet it had to be so, because she felt it in her heart. "Well," she said, more determinedly this time, "I'll make a terrific pastor's wife." She peered up into Mike's face. "Want to know why?"

"Sure," he answered, wearing an expectant grin.

She smiled broadly, knowing that what she was about to say came straight from her heart. "Because I love the pastor."

epilogue

Risa hugged her cousin. "Thanks for sharing your special day with me." She pulled back and gave Annamarie's attire two sweeping glances, studying the white, lacy tea-length gown and her cousin's dark hair pinned up and arrayed with baby's breath. "You look gorgeous."

"So do you. . .and I'm honored that you're sharing your special day with me too. Besides, Tony said it's only fair, since Mike was the one who convinced him to quit procrastinating and marry me."

Risa laughed, then smoothed down the skirt of her wedding dress. She still deemed it a miracle that she'd found this gown in stock—and it was on sale, no less. Similar to her cousin's, it was tea-length and not the traditional full gown. But that's what Risa had wanted—and that's why she'd loved Annamarie's gown so much.

"And you said *I* was being hasty, planning a wedding in three months," Annamarie chided her. "You planned yours in less than two weeks!"

"Everything just fell into place."

Another miracle.

Mike had secured Bay Community Church, which pleased Annamarie, who hadn't been all that thrilled with the wedding chapel idea. But since Annamarie and Tony weren't active members anywhere, they felt the chapel was their only option. However, Annamarie still got her wish to be married on Valentine's Day.

And Nana got her wish to have a formal sit-down meal afterward, again thanks to Mike. He knew a great Italian place with a banquet hall large enough to accommodate everyone.

Moreover, Risa's secret desire to be wed before her younger cousin would now be a reality too, sort of. . . . Actually, the "before" now was "with." But that meant little to Risa. She just felt so happy to be marrying the man she loved. In fact, she'd never been happier.

"Did you have any problems talking Kari's mother into watching Jodi for the next few days?"

Risa shook her head. "No, she agreed. And when Mike and I dropped Jodi off, we were able to discuss the possibility of adoption. Arlene promised to think about it and talk to José."

"Think they'll go along with it?" her cousin asked, smoothing a lovely shade of rose across her lips.

"Yeah, especially since Mike promised Arlene that she and the rest of Kari's family can see her anytime. Our intention isn't to rip Jodi away from her family. We just love her and want to provide the best home possible."

"You guys'll be terrific parents."

"Thanks." Risa grinned. "We think so too."

A knock sounded on the door and, still smiling over her last remark, she pulled it open. There, to Risa's surprise, stood Leslie Owens.

"Could I have a word with you?" Dressed in a navy skirt and light blue blouse, she smiled at Annamarie before glancing back to Risa. "What I have to say won't take but a minute."

"Sure." Stepping outside the small bridal chamber located adjacent to the sanctuary, Risa could only wonder what Leslie wanted. They'd been cordial to each other in recent weeks but hadn't had an opportunity for conversation. "What's up?"

"Well, first I want to say that you look stunning," Leslie began.

"Thanks," Risa said, meaning it.

"Next, I wanted to apologize."

"Forget it."

"No, I can't. You see, I ran ahead of the Lord by assuming He wanted me to marry Pastor Gerardi. I was so concerned with roadblocks in my way that I became one myself. I'm ashamed of how I behaved."

Tears welled in Leslie's eyes, melting Risa's heart. "All's forgiven," Risa said, giving the woman a hug.

"Thank you. You're. . .well, you're very compassionate. I have no doubt you'll make a wonderful pastor's wife." Leslie stepped back and sniffed. Then she lifted her chin. "Now if you'll excuse me, I'm in charge of the music for a certain wedding ceremony that will begin any moment."

"By all means, you're excused," Risa said with a laugh.

Leslie smiled, turned on her heel, and quickly strode off to the sanctuary.

Risa reentered the little chamber.

"Everything okay?" Annamarie asked.

"Everything's perfect."

"Good." Annamarie scrutinized Risa's face. "Here, you need some color," she said, handing over the tube of lipstick that she'd used minutes earlier.

Risa glanced in the mirror, applied the glossy rose to her lips, and then rubbed them together. Viewing her reflection, she was satisfied with the image returning her gaze. Her hair had been swept up and loosely pinned in back, while curly tendrils fell attractively around her face. Turning, Risa handed the tube to her cousin and grinned. "We even share lipstick."

Annamarie laughed softly and nodded before capping it and tucking it into her purse. At that moment, the door opened and both mothers entered.

"Okay, the bridesmaids are all lined up and have begun their walk down the aisle," Aunt Cathy said, her dark eyes shining. "Now it's your turn." She handed each woman a bouquet of red and white roses.

Risa's mother hugged her tightly. "I'm so happy for you, Honey. Mike is such a nice man."

"The nicest."

"Well, almost the nicest," Annamarie sweetly disagreed.

"Tony's not too bad himself."

With smiles of happiness on their faces, the group of four made its way into the foyer. Risa heard the organ playing the traditional bridal march and knew Leslie Owens sat at the keyboard. She had volunteered to organize the music, which included a touching arrangement sung by some of the teens at the church, including Mary Beth and Tracy.

"This is the most wonderful day of my life!" Annamarie declared as she stood poised and ready to meet her groom. She took hold of her father's arm, and seconds later they began their procession.

Risa looked at her dad and threaded her hand around his elbow. It had been decades since the Vitalis family and the Mandelinis had sat under the same roof. However, this wedding had brought them together. Many fences still needed repair, burned bridges needed rebuilding, but this was at least a start.

"You look like a million bucks," Nick Vitalis said, bending his dark head close to Risa's.

"Thanks, Dad." She gave his arm a loving squeeze.

Then it was time for their stroll to the altar.

Risa caught Mike's gaze. He stood off to the right, below the pulpit, waiting for her. The obvious anticipation he felt shone on his face.

She smiled at him.

He smiled back, causing her heart to soar.

And Risa knew that she had never before experienced such joy.

A Letter To Our Readers

Dear Reader:

In order that we might better contribute to your reading enjoyment, we would appreciate your taking a few minutes to respond to the following questions. We welcome your comments and read each form and letter we receive. When completed, please return to the following:

Rebecca Germany, Fiction Editor
Heartsong Presents
PO Box 719
Uhrichsville, Ohio 44683

1. Did you enjoy reading *Risa's Rainbow* by Andrea Boeshaar?
   ❑ Very much! I would like to see more books
   by this author!
   ❑ Moderately. I would have enjoyed it more if

   _____

   _____

   _____

2. Are you a member of **Heartsong Presents**? Yes ❑ No ❑
   If no, where did you purchase this book?_____

   _____

3. How would you rate, on a scale from 1 (poor) to 5 (superior), the cover design?_____

4. On a scale from 1 (poor) to 10 (superior), please rate the following elements.

   _____ Heroine   _____ Plot

   _____ Hero   _____ Inspirational theme

   _____ Setting   _____ Secondary characters

5. These characters were special because_____

   _____

   _____

6. How has this book inspired your life?_____

   _____

   _____

7. What settings would you like to see covered in future
   Heartsong Presents books?_____

   _____

   _____

8. What are some inspirational themes you would like to see
   treated in future books?_____

   _____

   _____

9. Would you be interested in reading other **Heartsong
   Presents** titles?   Yes ❑   No ❑

10. Please check your age range:
    ❑ Under 18   ❑ 18-24   ❑ 25-34
    ❑ 35-45   ❑ 46-55   ❑ Over 55

Name _____

Occupation _____

Address _____

City _____ State _____ Zip _____

Email _____

The Chalice of Israel

For nearly two thousand years a special ceremonial cup has changed the lives of Jews and Gentiles alike. Its beauty and aura of mystery compel those who hold it to seek out the meaning of its Hebrew inscription, "I will pour out my blood for you." For four young women of four separate eras, the cup holds a promise of courage, hope, honor, and praise.

Authors Marilou H. Flinkman, Susannah Hayden, Jane LaMunyon, and Darlene Mindrup.

paperback, 336 pages, 5 ³⁄₁₆" x 8"

Hearts♥ng

Any 12 Heartsong Presents titles for only $27.00*

CONTEMPORARY ROMANCE IS CHEAPER BY THE DOZEN!

Buy any assortment of twelve *Heartsong Presents* titles and save 25% off of the already discounted price of $2.95 each!

*plus $2.00 shipping and handling per order and sales tax where applicable.

Presents

__HP349 WILD TIGER WIND, *G. Buck*
__HP350 RACE FOR THE ROSES, *L. Snelling*
__HP353 ICE CASTLE, *J. Livingston*
__HP354 FINDING COURTNEY, *B. L. Etchison*
__HP357 WHITER THAN SNOW, *Y. Lehman*
__HP358 AT ARM'S LENGTH, *G. Sattler*
__HP361 THE NAME GAME, *M. G. Chapman*
__HP362 STACY'S WEDDING, *A. Ford*
__HP365 STILL WATERS, *G. Fields*
__HP366 TO GALILEE WITH LOVE, *E. M. Berger*
__HP370 TWIN VICTORIES, *C. M. Hake*
__HP373 CATCH OF A LIFETIME, *Y. Lehman*
__HP377 COME HOME TO MY HEART,
       J. A. Grote
__HP378 THE LANDLORD TAKES A BRIDE,
       K. Billerbeck
__HP381 SOUTHERN SYMPATHIES, *A. Boeshaar*
__HP382 THE BRIDE WORE BOOTS, *J. Livingston*
__HP390 LOVE ABOUNDS, *A. Bell*
__HP394 EQUESTRIAN CHARM, *D. Mills*
__HP401 CASTLE IN THE CLOUDS, *A. Boeshaar*
__HP402 SECRET BALLOT, *Y. Lehman*
__HP405 THE WIFE DEGREE, *A. Ford*
__HP406 ALMOST TWINS, *G. Sattler*
__HP409 A LIVING SOUL, *H. Alexander*
__HP410 THE COLOR OF LOVE, *D. Mills*
__HP413 REMNANAT OF VICTORY, *J. Odell*
__HP414 THE SEA BECKONS, *B. L. Etchison*
__HP417 FROM RUSSIA WITH LOVE, *C. Coble*

__HP418 YESTERYEAR, *G. Brandt*
__HP421 LOOKING FOR A MIRACLE,
       W. E. Brunstetter
__HP422 CONDO MANIA, *M. G. Chapman*
__HP425 MUSTERING COURAGE, *L. A. Coleman*
__HP426 TO THE EXTREME, *T. Davis*
__HP429 LOVE AHOY, *C. Coble*
__HP430 GOOD THINGS COME, *J. A. Ryan*
__HP433 A FEW FLOWERS, *G. Sattler*
__HP434 FAMILY CIRCLE, *J. L. Barton*
__HP437 NORTHERN EXPOSURE, *J. Livingston*
__HP438 OUT IN THE REAL WORLD, *K. Paul*
__HP441 CASSIDY'S CHARM, *D. Mills*
__HP442 VISION OF HOPE, *M. H. Flinkman*
__HP445 MCMILLIAN'S MATCHMAKERS,
       G. Sattler
__HP446 ANGELS TO WATCH OVER ME,
       P. Griffin
__HP449 AN OSTRICH A DAY, *N. J. Farrier*
__HP450 LOVE IN PURSUIT, *D. Mills*
__HP453 THE ELUSIVE MR. PERFECT, *T. H. Murray*
__HP454 GRACE IN ACTION, *K. Billerbeck*
__HP457 A ROSE AMONG THORNS, *L. Bliss*
__HP458 THE CANDY CANE CALABOOSE,
       J. Spaeth
__HP461 PRIDE AND PUMPERNICKEL, *A. Ford*
__HP462 SECRETS WITHIN, *G. G. Martin*
__HP465 TALKING FOR TWO, *W. E. Brunstetter*
__HP466 RISA'S RAINBOW, *Andrea Boeshaar*

Great Inspirational Romance at a Great Price!

Heartsong Presents books are inspirational romances in contemporary and historical settings, designed to give you an enjoyable, spirit-lifting reading experience. You can choose wonderfully written titles from some of today's best authors like Hannah Alexander, Irene B. Brand, Yvonne Lehman, Tracie Peterson, and many others.

When ordering quantities less than twelve, above titles are $2.95 each.
Not all titles may be available at time of order.

SEND TO: **Heartsong Presents** Reader's Service
P.O. Box 721, Uhrichsville, Ohio 44683

Please send me the items checked above. I am enclosing $_____
(please add $2.00 to cover postage per order. OH add 6.25% tax. NJ
add 6%.). Send check or money order, no cash or C.O.D.s, please.
To place a credit card order, call 1-800-847-8270.

NAME _____

ADDRESS _____

CITY/STATE_____ ZIP _____

HPS 1-02

Hearts♥ng Presents
Love Stories Are Rated G!

That's for godly, gratifying, and of course, great! If you love a thrilling love story but don't appreciate the sordidness of some popular paperback romances, **Heartsong Presents** is for you. In fact, **Heartsong Presents** is the *only inspirational romance book club* featuring love stories where Christian faith is the primary ingredient in a marriage relationship.

Sign up today to receive your first set of four never-before-published Christian romances. Send no money now; you will receive a bill with the first shipment. You may cancel at any time without obligation, and if you aren't completely satisfied with any selection, you may return the books for an immediate refund!

Imagine. . .four new romances every four weeks—two historical, two contemporary—with men and women like you who long to meet the one God has chosen as the love of their lives. . .all for the low price of $9.97 postpaid.

To join, simply complete the coupon below and mail to the address provided. **Heartsong Presents** romances are rated G for another reason: They'll arrive *Godspeed!*